Genoa

GENOA

A TELLING OF WONDERS

PAUL METCALF

UNIVERSITY OF

NEW MEXICO PRESS

ALBUQUERQUE

Design by Jonathan Williams
Cover illustration by Michael McCurdy
Cover design by Barbara Werden

Library of Congress Cataloging-in-Publication Data
Metcalf, Paul C.
Genoa : a telling of wonders / Paul Metcalf.
p.   cm.
Originally published: Penland, N.C. : Jargon Society, 1965.
ISBN 0-8263-1300-0
I. Title.
PS3563.E83G4   1991
813'.54—dc20   91-23293
CIP

CONTENTS

Genoa

HEADWATERS

ONE

City of Indianapolis, a cold spring day, late. Blackberry winter, my father called it—after some warm days, some affluence of sunshine, a sudden crackling blast of cold, rain edged with sleet, low, almost formless clouds scudding across the level land.

> *"When ocean clouds over inland hills*
> *Sweep storming . . ."*

Thus Herman Melville put it, thinking, perhaps of Pittsfield. Here there are no hills—only the squared-out city. Further south, toward the Ohio, Crawford County, where Mother's family, the Stoneciphers, came from, there are hills—hills and valleys, woods and caves.

But here I turn a square corner, and the old house comes into view, the house that used to be country and now is city, that has not moved, but in remaining still has allowed our fellow Americans to sweep around it, to put up suburban dwellings in what used to be the corn field, so that it now stands, as it ever was, but with the largeness of land lopped off; the house in which I was born and raised, on the land that we farmed; house and land that we lossed, or that I thought we had lossed, but that unknown to the rest of us remained, during the years of depression, in the arthritic grip of my mother, so that when I married and gave evidence of settling down, it fell into my lap, a gift —the land gone, but the rough old house, of timbers pegged and nailed before the Civil War, the house my father was born in, and his father before him, standing strong.

My father's name was Paul B. Mills—he would never tell us what the

1

B. stood for—we would guess and joke about it, Carl and I, but he remained passive and humourless—nor did my mother offer help, either condone or criticize our curiosity, and to this day I don't know if she ever discovered what it was—but there was the strange look from him one day when out of a clear blue, I had been thinking of other matters, I suddenly said "Bunyon—my father is Paul Bunyon," and again he neither affirmed nor denied, just for a moment the queer look—but there it was, on the birth certificate that showed up after his death, and the shock, perhaps greater than the accident of his death and those who died with him, the funeral, the relatives, the shock when I read it, the spelling of it: "Paul Bunion Mills."

Making the right angle turn I am now "running up into the wind's eye," as Melville said it—the only approach to a storm. Elbows digging into ribs hold an overcoat tight around me, and I lean forward, letting the rain and sleet beat against my face, so that forehead, cheeks, nose and chin, and the lines incised into my face, become a mask, at once me and not me, alive . . .

> "During the Cambrian, Ordovician, and most of the Silurian periods, Indiana was submerged beneath the seas. In the later Silurian, a mighty upheaval began; eventually most of the continent was uplifted and the great interior seas slowly receded. This was not a violent or sudden process; the earth rose only an inch, perhaps, in a century or more."

> "In the Mississippian and Pennsylvanian epochs of the Carboniferous period, Indiana was steadily elevated; at the close of the Mississippian the whole region was above sea level. During the Pennsylvanian, a period of millions of years, Indiana was probably a rank, lush swamp— populated by amphibious creatures, and covered with fern-like plants growing in vast luxuriance."

> "In the Pleistocene about five-sixths of the whole region—all except what is now south central Indiana—was at one time or another under a massive layer of ice, sometimes 2,000 feet thick."

and

The Miami, original Indian inhabitants of Indiana, lived on wild game and fowl, corn, tubers, roots and dogs. As late as 1812, the Miami burned their war captives, but the practice of cooking and eating them, which had once been very popular, ceased around 1789.

Passing the suburban houses, homogenized so that one might be another, I approach the old farm house down the road, anachronistic and stubborn; but for this, the regularity would be complete.

Complete, that is, but for one other factor, rendering irregular all that I reach through my eyes: with every step I lean off balance, off center, and back again, the prairie landscape ragging down with every leftward thrust:

Klumpfuss. Pied bot. Reel foot. Or, from the medical book: "Talipes equinovalgus, or 'rocker foot,' with some syndactilism." I have clubfoot.

From Melville, Mardi:

> "Averse to the barbarous custom of destroying at birth all infants not symmetrically formed; but equally desirous of removing from their sight those unfortunate beings; the islanders of a neighboring group had long ago established an asylum for cripples; where they lived, subject to their own regulations; ruled by a king of their own election; in short, formed a distinct class of beings by themselves.
>
> One only restriction was placed upon them: on no account must they quit the isle assigned them. And to the surrounding islanders, so unpleasant the sight of a distorted mortal, that a stranger landing at Hooloomooloo, was deemed a prodigy. Wherefore, respecting any knowledge of aught beyond them, the cripples were well nigh as isolated, as if Hooloomooloo was the only terra firma extant.
>
> Dwelling in a community of their own, these unfortunates, who otherwise had remained few in number, increased and multiplied greatly. Nor did successive generations improve in symmetry upon those preceding them.
>
> Soon, we drew nigh the isle.
>
> Heaped up, and jagged with rocks; and, here and there, covered with dwarfed, twisted thickets, it seemed a fit place for its denizens. Landing, we were surrounded by a heterogeneous mob; and thus escorted, took our way inland, toward the abode of their lord, King Yoky.
>
> What a scene!
>
> Here, helping himself along with two crotched roots, hobbled a dwarf without legs; another stalked before, one arm fixed in the air, like a lightning rod; a third, more active than any, seal-like, flirted a pair of flippers, and went skipping along; a fourth hopped on a solitary pin, at every bound, spinning around like a

3

top, to gaze; while still another, furnished with feelers or fins,
rolled himself up in a ball, bowling over the ground in advance."

The sleet cuts into my eyes, and I incise deeper the lines among the features, steel myself to the weather. Limping, steady-gaited, I turn into the path, past the frosted jonquils, leading to the door. The heavy latch responds.

"Oh, Daddy, Daddy—close the door, quick!"
Only one of my three children turns, the youngest, Jenifer.
And quickly her back is to me again, like the others.

As I stand just inside the closed door, shaking the weather from me, there is, first, the warmth of the house—central heating and therefore without source, simply a presence—then the second warmth, radiant from a source, and it is this that draws the family, as I felt drawn, as a child, to the black wood range, back in the kitchen: the family, now, the children, attentive to the glowing vacuum tube: the television. Taking off my coat, watching the hunched heads, the shoulders, the little backsides perched on stools, I think, for a moment,

> (*of Maria Melville, Herman Melville's
> mother, who, it is reliably reported, would
> require her eight children to sit on little stools
> around her bed, motionless, while she took
> her daily nap, that she might keep track of
> them*)

of the weird business, soon after we got the TV, of the electronic particles that hit the screen one night, and then kept recurring—I was in the kitchen, and the children came running, said there was a woman's face interfering with the cowboys—I recognized her from the show the night before—she stayed for a while, went away, and kept coming back—the service man tried to explain her, the local station, even the network people—none could give an answer, they had to take out the set, put in a new one.

Stepping into the kitchen, I reach at once for the oven

BECAUSE MY WIFE WORKS. I don't make enough money at General Motors to support the family—and it is this—this mystery, that my classmates at medical school are now making twenty, forty, fifty thousand a year, and I, possessing the same sheepskin, Doctor of

4

Medicine, and with a school record better actually than most of theirs, but the sheepskin is furled, in the attic, and I am unshingled, I cannot, will not practice, and this is mysterious to me

and so Linda works, going on the second shift at GM, already at her machine before I leave the first, and we have dates on the weekends. She cooks dinner before leaving home, puts it in the Frigidaire in warm weather, in the oven in cold, leaves the kids in care of the vacuum tube,

and I reach for the oven.

Now, there is a kind of ceremony about this, that I like. I, Michael Mills, presiding over the kitchen, the living room, the children, the house and grounds—a great chief, chef (of a meal already cooked), un jefe grande—Opening the oven door, lifting out the meat loaf and setting it on the stove, I stand for a moment, rubbing the five-o'clock stubble on the mandible, listening to the sounds of home (cowboy bullets) from the next room, and thinking

of Ushant, the old tar in White-Jacket *who survived the massacre of the beards—one of the people, merely, he held the hair of his chin, grimly, against the officers*

and of Melville's own—"no soft silken beard, but tight curled like the horse hair breaking out of old upholstered chairs, firm and wiry to the grasp, and squarely chopped."

and thinking, too, as the warm air from the open oven fills the room, of

Melville's daughter, Fanny, reporting him to be unhandy with tools, of no use around the house,

and thinking that, as common sailor on many a ship, he must have learned a certain handiness—but this he would not employ, to benefit the bark of domestic felicity *. . .*

and passing the meat loaf to the table, and the beans and the potatoes, from the top of the stove, there is a momentary recall, a pleasurable memory in the glands and the blood, of the three occasions when the children were born—I took leave from work and kept house while Linda was in the hospital, and each day, after cleaning, washing, making beds and taking in the milk, there was the ceremony of cooking dinner—made truly ceremonial, made ritual by the fact that, for a week, I grew a helluva ragged beard, and, as I cooked each evening, drank a glass of white port wine and smoked a black, child-destroying, outsize cigar

> *"Now, the leaf called tobacco is of diverse species and sorts. Not to dwell upon vile Shag, Pig-tail, Plug, Nail-rod, Negro-head, Cavendish, and misnamed Lady's twist . . ."*

Knowing better than to call the children before the commercials are over, I sit at the table and wait, warm and reminiscent. Then—we might have pickles, milk for the children, butter for beans and potatoes, and—a glance through the window at the steady dripping rain, the thick atmosphere—and

> *"ale must be drank in a fog and a drizzle."*

These from the Frigidaire to the table, and a swallow of ale inside; turning the bottle in my hand, and then staring at the jar of pickles, and my hand goes off the bottle and into my pocket, drawing forth a fragment of paper, before I think the connection. Shard of an old shopping list:

> **pickles**
> **&**
> **popsicles**

and a scribbling on the back, that I must have copied or added,

> **Pick-L-Joy**
> **&**
> **Popsie Pete**

> **"enclose the wrapper**
> **with twenty-five cen's**
> **and you will receive**
> **two ball point pens"**

The cowboy bullets have changed to talking cereal boxes, and I begin to serve the plates. In a moment, the children come to the table, and we have jokes, laughter, squabbles, scattered information, questions, jumping up and sitting down, a few tears, and—only casually and incidentally—the business of eating. Still, for all that,

a better temper than prevailed in the Melville household, where Herman would harangue his wife and two daughters (this was after the sons were gone) on matters that had no interest for them, and they would roll their eyes, and sigh, and wait, or there would be outbursts of temper, sarcasm

"Daddy, are we going to have a dessert tonight? A popsicle?"

There is an experience that I must try to understand, and it has to do with awareness, with a point in time and perhaps also in space where the awareness may be fixed, a time-space location, such as, say, a whale-ship, or perhaps what a cosmologist means when he says—with his stage the universe—"A fundamental observer partakes of the motion of the substratum, that is, he is located on a fundamental particle." Or, in my own terms, there is Carl, my brother, and the picture that flashes is Carl laughing, holding a book and laughing, and, at once, the illusion of hugeness, an illusion fostered, perhaps, by contrast with my own small frame, but shared nonetheless by others who also reported it, and it came not from height, for he was only five foot eight, but perhaps from a way of using himself, arrogant and careless, from a general stockiness of build, from a sultanic gluteus maximus, and, most of all, from the monstrous, out-shapen head that heaved and rolled with his mood, upon his shoulders. And it is all there, in this picture that flashed up from some back corner of my brain: the hugeness, a little of what Pliny meant when he said that "nature creates monsters for the purpose of astonishing us and amusing herself," and of the meaning of the word "Teratology," the medical term for the Science of Malformations and Monstrosities, from the Greek "teratologia," meaning "a telling of wonders." It is in the way his body and head shift, shake and revolve, as he laughs, as though composed of epicenters, randomly contiguous, with no single center, the parts loose, accidentally associated; it is in his hands, which are large hands, but again not as large as they appear from the way he uses them, the manner he has of holding the book, possessing it loosely, embracing it so as altogether to smother it, and at the same time letting it go loosely from his fingers, holding it at no single point, seeming to extend some of the casual humanity through his extremities into the very binding and paper, so that the pages flutter with the fierceness of the wings of a bird trapped, as he loses his place and finds it again, and quotes, from White-Jacket:

> "*I love an indefinite, infinite background—a vast, heaving, rolling, mysterious rear.*"

And again the burst of laughter, the explosion and re-shaping of his body, the unplanned and weirdly incomplete arcs described by his head,

7

the book squeezed and relinquished in one gesture. And as I hold this picture in my brain, this momentary recall—or as I am held by it—and add to it, bring along side it, the fact, the datum: Carl is dead, killed by gases released into a pan beneath his chair in the death chamber at Jefferson City, Missouri—this, his execution, being the last in a series of events as strangely associated as everything in his life, and which I still do not understand; when these—the image of him laughing, quoting, and the fact of his execution—are brought together, there is this experience, the fixing of my awareness at some time-space point that I am unable to identify, a seizure of elation

"My memory is a life beyond birth . . ."

Melville, in Mardi. And there is this: the time-space point is not limited to my own life-span, nor to the surfaces of the earth that I have traveled—nor are these areas excluded. My body feels dull, the blood slows, sensation withdraws from the extremities and consciousness, toward the trunk, and the meat loaf sits in ale, undigested in my stomach.

There is, after this, an illumination, an area of local bodily sensation, random and ephemeral, one following another, as a corollary, perhaps, an inscrutable hint, to the time-space fix itself—an intense warmth just above the heart, then something, an alertness, say, in the cells of the thigh; an ache in the shoulder, answered in a vertebra, and back again to the shoulder . . . and in the club, in the high, thick-soled boot, a tingling

"Daddy! Daddy!"

It is Jenifer, and her voice conveys alarm. I localize myself, search out the condition that she has discovered, and realize that, for some moments, I have been gazing at her, altogether oblivious to her. I glance for a moment at the room, open the senses: the old woodwork painted white, the warm air, the food smells. Turning to Jenifer—a smile, a word, a gesture, and she is restored. The dinner begins to move once more.

But eating I recall the medical student, interning in obstetrics, who made a custom of talking to newborn infants, presenting simple requests such as "open your eyes," "raise your right hand," or the like, and claimed remarkable results—the nurses liked to have him around, said he could quiet the most irritated or soothe the most feverish child;—pursuing his research, he developed a strange look, began to study philosophy and religion, and left medicine abruptly for divinity school.

One of the greatest pleasures of this house is the presence in it of the old chimney. In a fit of modernizing, Mother once wanted to cover it with wallboard, but I protested, successfully. A great mass of stone and mortar, it centers and roots the house; and, although all the fire-places except the one in the living-room have been sealed, portions of it appear, the stonework obtruding, refusing to be hidden, in nearly every room. Sitting at the table, now, observing the corner of it that appears in the kitchen, the sealed flue-opening before which the old black cookstove used to sit, I am reminded of Melville's I And My Chimney—and of the engineers, when we put in the furnace, telling me that the old chimney couldn't be used, a new one would have to be built, the flue wouldn't work—and of how I argued and persisted, with the result that now the stones impart flue heat—heat that would other-wise be wasted—to every room of the house, and even the long, narrow attic, running the length of the house, the attic where I keep my desk and books, the husbanding of Melville and medicine, history and archeology, even the attic is made livable, on a stormy spring night, by virtue of heat radiant from the old stones.

The children have begun the nightly chore of cleaning up the table and washing the dishes—spreading the job, fluctuant between dishwater and television. The day's manifest obligations having been met, it is not difficult for me to ascend the two flights to the attic—the heavy foot following the light, and then leading it—to meet, to face, to ex-amine, perhaps, some of the other obligations, such as

Item: a Post-mortem: to understand my brother Carl

and

Item: for the living, myself and others, to discover what it is to heal, and why, as a doctor, I will not.

T W O

"Save the prairie-hen, sometimes startled from its lurking-place in the rank grass; and, in their migratory season, pigeons, high overhead on the wing, in dense multitudes eclipsing the day like

a passing storm-cloud; save these—there being no wide woods with their underwood—birds were strangely few.

"Blank stillness would for hours reign unbroken on this prairie. 'It is the bed of a dried-up sea,' said the companionless sailor— no geologist—to himself, musing at twilight upon the fixed undulations of that immense alluvial expanse bounded only by the horizon, and missing there the stir that, to alert eyes and ears, animates at all times the apparent solitudes of the deep.

"But a scene quite at variance with one's antecedents may yet prove suggestive of them. Hooped round by a level rim, the prairie was to John Marr a reminder of ocean.

"With some of his former shipmates, chums on certain cruises, he had contrived, prior to this last and more remote removal, to keep up a little correspondence at odd intervals. But from tidings of anybody of any sort he, in common with the other settlers, was now cut off; quite cut off, except from such news as might be conveyed over the grassy billows by the last-arrived prairie-schooner —the vernacular term, in those parts and times, for the emigrant-wagon arched high over with sail-cloth, and voyaging across the vast champaign. There was no reachable post-office as yet; not even the rude little receptive box with lid and leather hinges, set up at convenient intervals on a stout stake along some solitary green way, affording a perch for birds, and which, later in the unremitting advance of the frontier, would perhaps decay into a mossy monument, attesting yet another successive overleaped limit of civilized life; a life which in America can to-day hardly be said to have any western bound but the ocean that washes Asia. Throughout these plains, now in places overpopulous with towns overopulent; sweeping plains, elsewhere fenced off in every direction into flourishing farms—pale townsmen and hale farmers alike, in part, the descendents of the first sallow settlers; a region that half a century ago produced little for the sustenance of man; but to-day launching its superabundant wheat-harvest on the world;—of this prairie, now everywhere intersected with wire and rail, hardly can it be said that at the period here written of there was so much as a traceable road. To the long-distance traveller the oak-groves, wide apart, and varying in compass and form; these, with recent settlements, yet more widely separate, offered some *landmarks; but otherwise he steered by the sun. In early mid-summer, even going but from one log-encampment to the next, a journey it might be of hours or good part of a day, travel was much like navigation. In some more enriched depressions be-tween the long, green, graduated swells, smooth as those of ocean becalmed receiving and subduing to its own tranquility the volu-minous surge raised by some far-off hurricane of days previous, here one would catch the first indication of advancing strangers either in the distance, as a far sail at sea, by the glistening white canvas of the wagon, the wagon itself wading through the rank vegetation and hidden by it, or, failing that, when near to, in the ears of the team, peeking, if not above the tall tiger-lilies, yet above the yet taller grass.*

"Luxuriant, this wilderness; but, to its denizen, a friend left be-hind anywhere in the world seemed not alone absent to sight, but an absentee from existence.

"Though John Marr's shipmates could not all have departed life, yet as subjects of meditation they were like phantoms of the dead. As the growing sense of his environment threw him more and more upon retrospective musings, these phantoms, next to those of his wife and child, became spiritual companions, losing some-thing of their first indistinctness and putting on at last a dim semblance of mute life; and they were lit by that aureola circling over any object of the affections in the past for reunion with which an imaginative heart passionately yearns."

Melville.

The dark oak rafters, forming the main roof gable of the house, are pitched low, so that there is only a narrow corridor, running east and west, of standing room, and this is flanked on either side by low-roofed shadows, filled with trunks, old furniture, magazines, and the like, things that Mother—though she survives in the nursing home down-town and knows she will never leave it—will not allow us to dispose of. Against the rock chimney is a makeshift desk—an old door, laid flat on crates—and running the length of this are the books—books that I have bought, found, begged throughout my life, ever since the morn-ing when Carl and I were playing in a haunted house, and we broke into what appeared to be a secret closet, discovered a small decanter of medicated sherry, the remnants of a whalebone corset, and an old copy of Typee. We rescued the whalebone from the rotted cloth, drank the sherry, and spent the rest of the day devouring what the bookworms had left of Typee.

Reaching the desk, I sit before it for a moment, uncritical, with perception undiminished, searching a balance.

> (*Melville, White-Jacket, called to observe a flogging: ". . . balanced myself on my best centre."*

There are the titles, the feel of an old binding: Mardi, for example, an early edition, in two volumes, dark brown, maroon, and black, the backing ribbed, and inside, the marbled end-papers, and the Preface:

> *"Not long ago, having published two narratives of voyages in the Pacific, which, in many quarters, were received with incredulity, the thought occurred to me, of indeed writing a romance of Polynesian adventure, and publishing it as such; to see whether, the fiction might not, possibly be received for a verity: in some degree the reverse of my previous experience."*

Then, Gray's Anatomy, Goss, Twenty-fifth Edition; and a disreputable copy of The Hoosier Schoolmaster, by Edward Eggleston. A thin, modern English book, Cosmology, by H. Bondi; The Search For Atlantis, by Edwin Bjorkman; and a copy of Natural History, March, 1952, including an article, Shrunken Heads. A Textbook Of Embryology, by Jordon and Kindred; also, Journal Of Morphology, Volume XIX, 1908, containing A Study Of The Causes Underlying The Origin Of Human Monsters.

Glancing upward, at the eight-inch rafters casting regular shadows across each other and across the roof boards, down the length of the attic, I am reminded

> *of the forecastle of the Julia in Omoo, planted "right in the bows, or, as sailors say, in the very eyes of the ship . . ."*

> *"All over, the ship was in a most dilapidated condition; but in the forecastle it looked like the hollow of an old tree going to decay. In every direction the wood was damp and discoloured, and here and there soft and porous. Moreover, it was hacked and hewed without mercy, the cook frequently helping himself to splinters for kindling-wood from the bitts and beams."*

and there was *"that gloomy hole where we burrowed like rabbits,"* in Redburn . . . as well as

The Gunner in White-Jacket—*". . . among all the persons and things on board that puzzled me, and filled me most with strange emotions of doubt, misgivings, and mystery, was the gunner—a short, square, grim man, his hair and beard grizzled and singed, as if with gunpowder. His skin was of a flecky brown, like the stained barrel of a fowling-piece, and his hollow eyes burned in his head like blue-lights. He it was who had access to many of those mysterious vaults I have spoken of. Often he might be seen groping his way into them . . ."*

and

". . . he was, withal, a very cross, bitter, illnatured, inflammable little old man. So, too, were all the members of the gunner's gang; including the two gunner's mates, and all the quarter-gunners. Every one of them had the same dark brown complexion; all their faces looked like smoked hams. They were continually grumbling and growling about the batteries; running in and out among the guns; driving the sailors away from them; and cursing and swearing as if all their consciences had been powder-singed and made callous by their calling. Indeed they were a most unpleasant set of men; especially Priming, the nasal-voiced gunner's mate, with the harelip; and Cylinder, his stuttering coadjutor, with the clubbed foot."

The wind rises, screaming faintly, intensely, against the north side, and the old house creaks.

"The hemlock shakes in the rafter, the oak in the driving keel."

and, in a letter, he (Melville)

"I have a sort of sea-feeling here in the country, now that the ground is covered with snow. I look out of my window in the morning when I rise as I would out of a port-hole of a ship in the Atlantic. My room seems a ship's cabin; & at nights when I wake up & hear the wind shrieking, I almost fancy there is too much sail in the house, & I had better go on the roof and rig in the chimney."

and again, at another season,

13

"In summer, too, Canute-like: sitting here, one is often reminded of the sea. For not only do long ground-swells roll the slanting grain, and little wavelets of the grass ripple over upon the low piazza, as their beach, and the blown down of dandelions is wafted like the spray, and the purple of the mountains is just the purple of the billows, and a still August noon broods upon the deep meadows, as a calm upon the Line; but the vastness and the lonesomeness are so oceanic, and the silence and the sameness, too, that the first peep of a strange house, rising beyond the trees, is for all the world like spying, on the Barbary coast, an unknown sail."

Glancing again at the rafters, I think of my great-grandfather, who built this house with his own hands: Hammond Mills, a yankee, born in New York City, who went up-river to Albany, and then west to Ohio and Indiana—a serious, hard-working man, whose favorite saying, his philosophy, perhaps, was handed down carefully from generation to generation, with the old furniture:

"The Mind is to the Body as the Whole Man is to the Earth."

> *(and there is Melville, Mardi: "We have had vast developments of parts of men; but none of manly wholes."*

Hammond Mills built this house, acquired the land, and farmed it. His first-born son, by the law of primogeniture, inherited and continued farming, passing on in turn to his first-born son: my father; and

Father married a Stonecipher, poor white, southerner. Her people came over from England as bond servants, landed somewhere on the coast, say Charleston, worked out their time and then worked gradually inland, keeping the mountains to the west until Boone had shown the way; then moving through the Gap, to the Ohio, down as far as Injeanny, where they settled in Brown and Crawford counties, started little hill farms, and hung on when many of the others continued west to Pike County, Missouri, and thence to California, as Pikers . . .

Greasy Creek, Gnaw Bone, and Shake Rag Hollow—the hills, ridges, knolls and bluffs to the north of the river—this is where the Stoneciphers dug in—farming, hunting, brawling, making likker—and later, in the flatboat era, moving down the Ohio and the Wabash, "half alligator and half horse, with a tech of wildcat" . . . but always, back to the farm, the root.

The folklore, too, came with the Stoneciphers:

Cut fence rails in the light of the moon, butcher before the full moon if the meat is to fry hard. Soap is to be made in the light of the moon, and stirred one way by one person. A waning moon is good for shingling, because it pulls the shingles flat.

and

A girl should never marry until she can pick clothes out of boiling water with her fingers, and if she sits on a table she will never marry. If a person kills a toad, his cow will give bloody milk.

And there was other folklore, too. Mother, hard-working, proud of the little cleanliness and respectability she could muster for us, quick with the flat of her hand when Carl or I misused the language, nevertheless used one word for all occasions, a word as old as words, ancient Anglo-Saxon association of four letters: shit. I have seen her dressed in her one good dress, serving tea for the preacher and his wife, and the word would come out, hang there in the middle of the room, unadorned and unexplained: and Mother would continue pouring.

After Father died, Carl left school, and, for a while, worked as a lumberjack in the Pacific Northwest; Mother was nearly frantic, he was gone for months and months, without sending word. Finally there was a postcard, undated and unsigned, but in his handwriting:

> Drink gin after cutting oak;
> bourbon follows pine.

This was all, for more than a year. He came home one day, "to get more winter clothes," as he said. He had joined an archeological expedition, persuading some college men of his erudition in Indian lore: in a few days—after delivering a lecture to Mother and me on the origins of American civilization—he was off to Alaska and the Aleutians,

"to dig boneyards in the Rat Islands."

Again, there was no word for months. Then there began to arrive, not cards or letters, but weird objects, drawings, fragments of stone and bone. A piece of steatite, apparently carved by Carl himself, in the shape of a killer whale; a section of human skull, occipital, huge, larger than Carl's own; a carving of an Indian woman, seated, with a symmetrical opening in her abdomen in which appeared a face, with a pair of huge, fierce eyes.

15

He was back again after several months, with more wild objects—and stories, in which, as Melville said, "fact and fancy, halfway meeting, interpenetrate, and form one seamless whole."

There was the shrunken human head, from the headwaters of the Amazon, which he admitted to having won from a fellow-archeologist in a poker game;

his story of a day's work carrying human remains from the cave where they were discovered, across the rocky, treacherous terrain, in a rainstorm, racing against the tide, to the boat—the description, with gestures, of picking up a bag of bones, the feeling of holding it in his arms, of having to hurry, with great delicacy, over the wet rocks, cradling the empty, formless treasures; and

the obscure tale of cannibalism, told when Carl was drunk, part of which seemed to take place a thousand years ago and involve Indians, and part of which took place just recently and involved Carl—something to do with eating a human being, genitals and extremities first, then the internal organs, flesh of the trunk, the neck, and finally the head—but the eyes! (and here Carl's eyes became wild) he couldn't eat the eyes!—or he did eat them and couldn't forget them, they haunted him, went straight to the brain, clinging to the lobes like barnacles to a ship's hull . . . and the feeling of holding only the skull in his hand, the eyes gone . . .

Olson:

> "Herman Melville was born in New York, August 1, 1819, and on the 12th of that month the Essex, a well-found whaler of 238 tons, sailed from Nantucket with George Pollard, Jr. as captain, Owen Chase and Matthew Joy mates, 6 of her complement of 20 men Negroes, bound for the Pacific Ocean, victualled and provided for two years and a half.
> "A year and three months later, on November 20, 1820, just south of the equator in longitude 119 West, this ship, on a calm day, with the sun at east, was struck head on twice by a bull whale, a spermaceti about 85 feet long, and with her bows stove in, filled and sank.
> "Her twenty men set out in three open whaleboats for the coast of South America 2000 miles away. They had bread (200 lb. a boat), water (65 gallons), and some Galapagos turtles. Although they were at the time no great distance from Tahiti, they were ignorant of the temper of the natives and feared cannibalism."

and

> "The three boats, with the seventeen men divided among them, moved

16

under the sun across ocean together until the 12th of January when, during the night, the one under the command of Owen Chase, First Mate, became separated from the other two.

"Already one of the seventeen had died,'Matthew Joy, Second Mate. He had been buried January 10th. When Charles Shorter, Negro, out of the same boat as Joy, died on January 23rd, his body was shared among the men of that boat and the Captain's, and eaten. Two days more and Lawson Thomas, Negro, died and was eaten. The bodies were roasted to dryness by means of fires kindled on the ballast sand at the bottom of the boats."

Thus, Herman Melville was born . . .

"*. . . which joyous event occured at ½ past 11 last night—our dear Maria displayed her accustomed fortitude in the hour of peril, & is as well as circumstances & the intense heat will admit —while the little Stranger has good lungs, sleeps well & feeds kindly, he is in truth a chopping Boy—*"

But there is more to this, to the birth of Herman: what is it about legs that so possessed the later man? Age twenty-one, the father dead, the family without funds, Herman unpaid for a year's teaching, and unemployed, shipped on a whaler for the Pacific, and thus broke away from home; but reaching the Marquesas, he again broke away, deserting ship on the island of Nukahiva, and thus doubly escaped, twice radically changed his world; and, at the entrance to the valley of Typee,

"*I began to feel symptoms which I at once attributed to the exposure of the preceding night. Cold shiverings and a burning fever succeeded one another at intervals, while one of my legs was swelled to such a degree, and pained me so acutely, that I half suspected I had been bitten by some venomous reptile . . .*"

And subsequently, the leg swelled and pained him whenever he thought or acted to escape from the Typees, subsiding when he was content with his life there; the leg saying to him—or he to himself—I cannot move.

Again, in Omoo, confined to the stocks in the Calabooza Beretanee (British Jail):

"*How the rest managed, I know not; but, for my own part, I found it very hard to get asleep. The consciousness of having one's foot pinned; and the impossibility of getting it anywhere else*" *than just where it was, was most distressing.*

"But this was not all: there was no way of lying but straight on your back; unless, to be sure, one's limb went round and round in the ankle, like a swivel. Upon getting into a sort of doze, it was no wonder this uneasy posture gave me the nightmare. Under the delusion that I was about some gymnastics or other, I gave my unfortunate member such a twitch, that I started up with the idea that some one was dragging the stocks away."

Or, in White-Jacket, the amputation performed by Dr. Cuticle:

". . . and then the top-man seemed parted in twain at the hip, as the leg slowly slid into the arms of the pale, gaunt man in the shroud, who at once made away with it, and tucked it out of sight under one of the guns."

(Note: how Melville hated doctors!

And in Moby-Dick, there is Captain Peleg (Pegleg) addressing young Ishmael:

" 'Dost see that leg?—I'll take that leg away from thy stern . . .' "

And Ahab:

"So powerfully did the whole grim aspect of Ahab affect me, and the livid brand which streaked it, that for the first few moments I hardly noted that not a little of this overbearing grimness was owing to the barbaric white leg upon which he partly stood. It had previously come to me that this ivory leg had at sea been fashioned from the polished bone of the sperm whale's jaw. 'Aye, he was dismasted off Japan,' said the old Gay-Head Indian once; 'but like his dismasted craft, he shipped another mast without coming home for it. He has a quiver of 'em.' "

and

"His three boats stove around him, and oars and men both whirling in the eddies; one captain, seizing the lineknife from his broken prow, had dashed at the whale, as an Arkansas duellist at his foe, blindly seeking with a six-inch blade to reach the fathom-deep life of the whale. That captain was Ahab. And then it was, that suddenly sweeping his sickle-shaped lower jaw beneath him, Moby-Dick had reaped away Ahab's leg, as a mower a blade of grass in the field."

18

August 1, 1819, New York City, a hot, dark night: Maria Melville, Herman's mother, has, for the third time, gone down into the valley, and Herman, still unborn, struggling in the Dardanelles, the Narrows of a white woman, and perhaps, like the baby whales, "still spiritually feasting upon some unearthly reminiscence"—Herman dies, to the extent that all life, all vitality retreats trunkward from one leg:—and then the "chopping Boy" is born.

> "... *deep memories yield no epitaphs." And yet, somewhere lies the thought: one must die to be born.*

Pierre:

> *"And here it may be randomly suggested . . . whether some things men think they do not know, are not for all that thoroughly comprehended by them; and yet, so to speak, though contained in themselves, are kept a secret from themselves? The idea of Death seems such a thing."*

Israel Potter:

> *"It was not the pang of hunger then, but a nightmare originating in his mysterious incarceration, which appalled him. All through the long hours of this particular night, the sense of being masoned up in the wall, grew, and grew, and grew upon him . . . he stretched his two arms sideways, and felt as if coffined at not being able to extend them straight out, on opposite sides, for the narrowness of the cell . . . He mutely raved in the darkness."*

White-Jacket:

> *"Just then the ship gave another sudden jerk, and, head foremost, I pitched from the yard. I knew where I was, from the rush of the air by my ears, but all else was a nightmare . . .*
>
> *"As I gushed into the sea, a thunder-boom sounded in my ear; my soul seemed flying from my mouth. The feeling of death flooded over me with the billows . . .*
>
> *"For one instant an agonizing revulsion came over me as I found myself utterly sinking. Next moment the force of my fall was expended; and there I hung, vibrating in the mid-deep. What wild sounds then rang in my ear! One was a soft moaning, as of low waves on the beach; the other wild and heartlessly jubilant, as of the sea in the height of a tempest . . . The life-and-death poise*

soon passed; and then I found myself slowly ascending, and caught a dim glimmering of light."

Perhaps on that hot night in August, 1819, the unborn Herman lingered like Queequeg in his coffin,

> (a rehearsal of death that was all the cure the savage needed . . .

> (the same coffin, the death-box—unhinged from the sunken whaler—on which Ishmael ultimately survived . . .

And we have this: the great, white, humped monster, that dismasted Ahab:

> *"Judge, then, to what pitches of inflamed, distracted fury the minds of his more desperate hunters were impelled, when amid the chips of chewed boats, and the sinking limbs of torn comrades, they swam out of the white curds of the whale's direful wrath into the serene, exasperating sunlight, that smiled on, as if at a birth . . ."*

There is again a split, a division of awareness, as earlier, at the dinner table, and for some time I am still, aware of my stillness, aware of my surroundings, of the Nineteenth-century attic whose dark, sloping lines seem an extension of frontal and parietal bones of the skull itself—aware that my attention is wandering, or perhaps fixed but inaccessible, and aware that this condition must be allowed to play itself out . . .

There being division, I am able to observe myself, to be at once within and without, and an exploration occurs, inwardly derived, over the surfaces, the topography of face and head, and downward over my body; I gain the sense of being different, of causing this difference in myself, of altering the outwardness of myself. I discover that flesh and muscle, perhaps even bone, and certainly cartilage, are potentially alterable, according as the plan is laid down. And the plan itself may shift and change: I may be this Michael or that, Stonecipher or Mills—Western Man or Indian, sea-dog or lubber, large-headed or small, living then or now; and even such outrageous fables as that of converting Ulysses' men into swine become not unreasonable, when we understand that the men must have experienced some swinish designs within themselves, to which Circe had access . . .

Certainly, the study of Man : Literature is the study of Man : Anatomy

. . . when it ceases to be, books become merely literary.

(Melville: "I rejoice in my spine."

Leaning back in the chair, my body straight out, I let the awareness sweep, as a tide, through my trunk, down my legs and into my feet.

Ahab: ". . . I'll order a complete man after a desirable pattern. Imprimus, fifty feet high in his socks; then, chest modelled after the Thames Tunnel; then, legs with roots to 'em, to stay in one place . . ."

and, with the carpenter,

"Look ye, carpenter, I dare say thou callest thyself a right good workmanlike workman, eh? Well, then, will it speak thoroughly well for thy work, if, when I come to mount this leg thou makest, I shall nevertheless feel another leg in the same identical place with it; that is, carpenter, my old lost leg; the flesh and blood one, I mean. Canst thou not drive that old Adam away?

"Truly, sir, I begin to understand somewhat now. Yes, I have heard something curious on that score, sir; how that a dismasted man never entirely loses the feeling of his old spar, but it will be still pricking him at times. May I humbly ask if it be really so, sir?

"It is, man. Look, put thy live leg here in the place where mine was; so, now, here is only one distinct leg to the eye, yet two to the soul. Where thou feelest tingling life; there, exactly there, to a hair, do I. Is't a riddle?

"I should humbly call it a poser, sir.

"Hist, then. How dost thou know that some entire, living, thinking thing may not be invisibly and uninterpenetratingly standing precisely where thou now standest; aye, and standing there in thy spite? In thy most solitary hours, then, dost thou not fear eavesdroppers?"

A sudden fury lashes me, a desire to mutilate myself, to amputate the great, round, ugly globe of a clubfoot—to make it not me. As in Mardi, in the chapter Dedicated To The College Of Physicians And Surgeons,

"In Polynesia, every man is his own barber and surgeon, cutting off his beard or arm, as occasion demands. No unusual thing, for the warriors . . . to saw off their own limbs, desperately wounded in battle . . ."

21

and

> *"The wound was then scorched, and held over the smoke of the fire, till all signs of blood vanished. From that day forward it healed, and troubled Samoa but little.*
>
> *"But shall the sequel be told? How that, superstitiously averse to burying in the sea the dead limb of a body yet living; since in that case Samoa held, that he must very soon drown and follow it; and how, that equally dreading to keep the thing near him, he at last hung it aloft from the topmast-stay; where yet it was suspended, bandaged over and over in cerements . . .*
>
> *"Now, which was Samoa? The dead arm swinging high as Haman? Or the living trunk below? Was the arm severed from the body, or the body from the arm? The residual part of Samoa was alive, and therefore we say it was he. But which of the writhing sections of a ten times severed worm, is the worm proper?"*

The fury lingers, contorting, aggravating . . .

> *"Small reason was there to doubt, then, that ever since that almost fatal encounter, Ahab had cherished a wild vindictiveness against the whale, all the more fell for that in his frantic morbidness he at last came to identify with him, not only all his bodily woes, but all his intellectual and spiritual exasperations. The White Whale swam before him as the monomaniac incarnation of all those malicious agencies which some deep men feel eating in them, till they are left living on with half a heart and half a lung."*

and there was the woman in the mental hospital, brought onto the platform in the lecture hall to demonstrate for the medical students, of which I was one:—she suffered with a compulsion to strip her ragged clothes, and over and over to lash herself . . .

The anger quiets a little, becoming sardonic, and then wrying into a smile. Again, there is Ahab:

> *". . . for this hunt, my malady becomes my most desired health."*

And Melville himself, reading of a writer whose work was presumed to be influenced by his illness, makes a marginal comment:

> *"So is every one influenced—the robust, the weak, all constitutions —by the very fibre of the flesh, & chalk of the bone. We are what we were made."*

Rising, I turn from the desk, and begin to walk, without aim, but confined by the structure of the attic itself. I think again of the infant Melville, held motionless through a brain-caking hiatus, before his delivery; and then of myself, and of the medical data regarding Talipes:

The notion that heredity may not be a factor; that, more likely, clubfoot results from the maintenance of a strained position in the uterus, or entanglement with the cord, or interlocking of the feet . . .

And further:

> "*Equinus—The heel cord and the posterior structures of the leg are contracted, holding the foot in plantarflection. The arch of the foot is abnormally elevated into cavus and weight is borne on the ball of the foot. In infancy, correction may be accomplished by successive plasters gradually forcing the foot into dorsiflexion. It is extremely important that the cavus, or high arch, be corrected before the cord is lengthened. It may be necessary to sever the contracted structures on the sole of the foot. These consist principally of the plantar fascia and short toe flexors. These structures may be divided subcutaneously. After the cavus deformity has been completely corrected, the heel cord may be lengthened by tenotomy or successive plaster.*"

> "*Valgus—In early infancy, the foot should be manipulated daily by the mother, twisting it into a position of adduction and inversion. A light aluminum splint should be worn day and night to maintain correction. . . . After care consists in the wearing of a Thomas heel and special exercises to develop the anticus, posticus and toe flexors.*"

I have observed these operations and manipulations, performed on others; but in my own case, things being as they were, none of this was done.

The westward end of the attic, farthest removed from the chimney, is cold, and I hear the rain against the side of the house. I turn, and amble back to the desk.

"I was struck with the singular position he maintained. Upon each side of the Pequod's quarter deck, and pretty close to the mizzen shrouds, there was an auger hole, bored about half an inch or so, into the plank. His bone leg steadied in that hole; one arm elevated, and holding by a shroud; Captain Ahab stood erect, looking straight out beyond the ship's ever-pitching prow. There was an infinity of firmest fortitude, a determinate, unsurrenderable willfulness, in the fixed and fearless, forward dedication of that glance."

But my foot finds no auger holes, and if bare, would roll like a globe on the old planks.

Reaching the desk, I sit down, body straight out as before, head tilted back . . .

"But that night, in particular, a strange (and ever since inexplicable) thing occurred to me. Starting from a brief standing sleep, I was horribly conscious of something fatally wrong. The jawbone tiller smote my side, which leaned against it; in my ears was the low hum of sails, just beginning to shake in the wind; I thought my eyes were open; I was half conscious of putting my fingers to the lids and mechanically stretching them still further apart. But, in spite of all this, I could see no compass before me to steer by; though it seemed but a minute since I had been watching the card, by the steady binnacle lamp illuminating it. Nothing seemed before me but a jet gloom, now and then made ghastly by flashes of redness. Uppermost was the impression, that whatever swift, rushing thing I stood on was not so much bound to any haven ahead as rushing from all havens astern. A stark, bewildered feeling, as of death, came over me. Convulsively my hands grasped the tiller, but with the crazy conceit that the tiller was, somehow, in some enchanted way, inverted. My God! what is the matter with me? thought I. Lo! in my brief sleep I had turned myself about, and was fronting the ship's stern, with my back to her prow and the compass."

My eyes suddenly grow dim. I am, in effect, under water, my vision snuffing out like candle flames. I am rigid, but alive, aware.

There is a sense of motion, barely perceptible, yet abrupt; motion neither within nor around me, but something of both . . .

like the cadaverous man in the mental hospital, haggard with sleeplessness, who fixed a rigid grip on his bedposts every night, "to keep from slipping away" . . .

or Melville in Omoo, feet in the stocks, waking with the notion of being dragged . . .

or perhaps like an old sea captain, comfortably resting in his home ashore, startled by the thought of the house pitching . . .

> *"It is not probable that this monomania in him took its instant rise at the precise time of his bodily dismemberment. Then, in darting at the monster, knife in hand, he had but given loose to a sudden, passionate, corporal animosity; and when he received the stroke that tore him, he probably but felt the agonizing bodily laceration, but nothing more. Yet, when by this collision forced to turn towards home, and for long months of days and weeks, Ahab and anguish lay stretched together in one hammock, rounding in mid winter that dreary, howling Patagonian Cape; then it was, that his torn body and gashed soul bled into one another . . ."*

I am covered from head to foot, unable to move, a small boy, standing upright; I taste dirt on my lips. There is a moment of amnesia, and, separate from this, the knowledge that the bottoms of my feet hurt, and the lower spine and back of the head have been jolted. Then, the recognition, the discovery: I have fallen, with arms pinned to my body, into the empty post-hole, around the edges of which I had a moment before been playing.

With this recognition comes the experience: I had wandered from Carl, discovered the freshly dug holes along the edge of the field, had inspected them one after another, skipping over them, leaning into them, dropping pebbles in, and finally, reaching the last and loneliest, farthest from the house, had slipped on the clubfoot, and, as in burial of a sailor died at sea, had slid beneath the surface and out of sight.

The modified sensations linger in my body, still rigid in the chair, as more of the emotion comes back: the desolation and helplessness, the abandonment; the stopping of time, and, in its place, a circular expansion of sensation, a vortex in reverse, limitless in proportion to my physical confinement. Almost dizzy, I am not at first aware of the shadow that moves over my head, or even of my father's hands slipping under my arms to lift me out. It is only the merest chance that he decided to survey his day's digging, and heard my cries.

Worse than the accident itself were the cold pity I received, the assumption, without asking, that the "bad" foot was to blame, and my own knowledge that this and only this saved me from punishment . . .

There was, too, the nature of the accident, the ignominy of it; especially as it came soon after Carl's more dramatic tumble out of the haymow, twelve feet to the concrete floor of the barn . . .

> (*We had been playing in the hay, and when I ducked suddenly, he lunged past me and over the edge. I looked up and watched him fall: he landed flat on his back, his rump, shoulderblades and back of his head taking the blow; he appeared to bounce, the act of rising being continuous with that of falling, so that he was for a moment off the floor again, landing the second time on his feet, and emitting two single words,*

> **"JESUS CHRIST!"**

> *that my father claimed to have heard at the far end of the corn field, half a mile away.*

> (*He staggered for a moment, and shook himself—the motion originating in his buttocks, and rising loosely through his torso, until finally his great head rocked and shivered; then he glanced at me, and, for an instant, there was a queer smile, at once large-hearted and derisive, and a look in his eye that understood and conveyed more than he could speak. Then he raced for the ladder, and a moment later we were playing again in the hay, the accident ignored.*

My body relaxes a little, releases itself, unwilling to participate further in the work of the mind. Other images, however, come flashing in . . .

I see Carl, age twelve, the time he found a bottle of gin, and got himself fabulously drunk. No longer able to stand, he suddenly discovered that he could roll the pupils of his eyes in little circles, and could control the motion: rolling them first one way then the other, clockwise and counter-clockwise; then rolling one eye at a time, while the other was still; rolling both at once, each in a different direction; then reversing the directions. This gave him an idiotic satisfaction, and he continued until he passed out, going to sleep without ever lowering his eyelids, so that when he was snoring, I could still see the naked eyes, free of design and volition, meandering . . .

Now I see him swimming, going under the surface to take in a mouthful of water, then coming up, floating on his back, his body all belly and head in profile, while he spouts a great long stream of water, so that it seems he must have the whole lake in his head.

> *"But as the colossal skull embraces so very large a proportion of the entire extent of the skeleton . . ."*

Melville, speaking of the sperm whale; and

> *"It does seem to me, that herein we see the rare virtue of a strong individual vitality, and the rare virtue of thick walls, and the rare virtue of interior spaciousness. Oh, man! admire and model thyself after the whale!"*

and

> *"If you unload his skull of its spermy heaps and then take a rear view of its rear end, which is the high end, you will be struck by its resemblance to the human skull, beheld in the same situation, and from the same point of view. Indeed, place this reversed skull (scaled down to the human magnitude) among a plate of men's skulls, and you would involuntarily confound it with them . . ."*

Now it is Carl coming at me, in mock fierceness, when we are roughhousing. He imitates a professional wrestler, ape-like, all arms and shoulders, with the illusion not only of having no neck, but of his head actually being sunk in his body—a round, weather-smooth rock wedged in a cleft between boulders.

> *"If you attentively regard almost any quadruped's spine, you will be struck with the resemblance of its vertebrae to a strung necklace of dwarfed skulls, all bearing rudimental resemblance to the skull proper. It is a German conceit, that the vertebrae are absolutely undeveloped skulls. But the curious external resemblance, I take it the Germans were not the first men to perceive. A foreign friend once pointed it out to me, in the skeleton of a foe he had slain, and with the vertebrae of which he was inlaying, in a sort of basso-*

relievo, the beaked prow of his canoe. Now, I consider that the phrenologists have omitted an important thing in not pushing their investigations from the cerebellum through the spinal canal. For I believe that much of a man's character will be found betokened in his backbone . . .

"Apply this spinal branch of phrenology to the Sperm Whale. His cranial cavity is continuous with the first neck-vertebra; and in that vertebra the bottom of the spinal canal will measure ten inches across, being eight in height, and of a triangular figure with the base downwards. As it passes through the remaining vertebrae the canal tapers in size, but for a considerable distance remains of large capacity. Now, of course, this canal is filled with much the same strangely fibrous substance—the spinal cord—as the brain; and directly communicates with the brain. And what is still more, for many feet after emerging from the brain's cavity, the spinal cord remains of an undecreasing girth, almost equal to that of the brain. Under all these circumstances, would it be unreasonable to survey and map out the whale's spine phrenologically? For, viewed in this light, the wonderful smallness of his brain proper is more than compensated by the wonderful comparative magnitude of his spinal cord."

Melville, and the leviathanic unconscious . . .

Carl the wrestler fades, and his huge head approaches, blocking the sun. There is a moment of terror before the image finds its frame . . . Carl is leaving for the summer, to work on an uncle's farm, and we are standing on the front steps, late afternoon. Mother is standing over us, insisting that, as brothers, we should kiss, full on the lips, before parting. She places a firm hand on the back of each neck. Carl acquiesces somberly, and his head approaches, a great purple shadow without features, a giant eggplant. I shrink from the contact, narrowing my mouth to an incision—and his kiss descends on me, a wet plum.

"It should not have been omitted that previous to completely stripping the body of the leviathan, he was beheaded. Now, the beheading of the Sperm Whale is a scientific anatomical feat, upon which experienced whale surgeons very much pride themselves: and not without reason.

"Consider that the whale has nothing that can properly be called a neck; on the contrary, where his head and body seem to

28

join, there, in that very place, is the thickest part of him. Remember, also, that the surgeon must operate from above, some eight or ten feet intervening between him and his subject, and that subject almost hidden in a discolored, rolling, and oftentimes tumultuous and bursting sea. Bear in mind, too, that under these untoward circumstances he has to cut many feet deep in the flesh; and in that subterraneous manner, without so much as getting one single peep into the ever-contracting gash thus made, he must skilfully steer clear of all adjacent, interdicted parts, and exactly divide the spine at a critical point hard by its insertion into the skull. Do you not marvel, then, at Stubb's boast, that he demanded but ten minutes to behead a sperm whale?

"When first severed, the head is dropped astern and held there by a cable till the body is stripped. That done, if it belong to a small whale it is hoisted on deck to be deliberately disposed of. But, with a full grown leviathan this is impossible; for the sperm whale's head embraces nearly one third of his entire bulk, and completely to suspend such a burden as that, even by the immense tackles of a whaler, this were as vain a thing as to attempt weighing a Dutch barn in jeweller's scales."

There is this about Carl: all the evidence indicates that he was conceived out of wedlock. There was the hasty wedding, and his birth in less than the full time thereafter. Mother's only comment was that he was a fast baby, but perhaps that's the way she wished to think of him. The only mystery to me is that she ever consented to conceive and bear another—myself—after the time she must have had in delivering Carl.

There was Tashtego, dipping sperm oil by the bucketful from the whale's head:

". . . but, on a sudden, as the eightieth or ninetieth bucket came suckingly up—my God! poor Tashtego—like the twin reciprocating bucket in a veritable well, dropped head-foremost down into this great Tun of Heidelburgh, and with a horrible oily gurgling, went clean out of sight!

.   .   .   .

" 'Stand clear of the tackle!' cried a voice like the bursting of a rocket.

"Almost in the same instant, with a thunder-boom, the enormous mass dropped into the sea, like Niagara's Table-Rock into

the whirlpool; the suddenly relieved hull rolled away from it, to far down her glittering copper; and all caught their breath, as half swinging—now over the sailors' heads and now over the water— Daggoo, through a thick mist of spray, was dimly beheld clinging to the pendulous tackles, while poor, buried-alive Tashtego was sinking utterly down to the bottom of the sea! But hardly had the blinding vapor cleared away, when a naked figure with a boarding sword in his hand, was for one swift moment seen hovering over the bulwarks. The next a loud splash announced that my brave Queequeg had dived to the rescue. One packed rush was made to the side, and every one counted every ripple, as moment followed moment, and no sign of either the sinker or the diver could be seen. Some hands now jumped into a boat alongside, and pushed a little off from the ship.

" 'Ha! ha!' cried Daggoo, all at once, from his now quiet, swinging perch overhead; and looking further off from the side, we saw an arm thrust upright from the blue waves; a sight strange to see, as an arm thrust forth from the grass over a grave.

" 'Both! both!—it is both!'—cried Daggoo again with a joyful shout; and soon after, Queequeg was seen striking out with one hand, and with the other clutching the long hair of the Indian. Drawn into the waiting boat, they were quickly brought to the deck; but Tashtego was long in coming to, and Queequeg did not look very brisk.

"Now, how had this noble rescue been accomplished? Why, diving after the slowly descending head, Queequeg with his keen sword had made side lunges near its bottom, so as to scuttle a large hole there; then dropping his sword, had thrust his long arm far inwards and upwards, and so hauled out poor Tash by the head. He averred, that upon first thrusting in for him, a leg was presented; but well knowing that that was not as it ought to be, and might occasion great trouble;—he had thrust back the leg, and by a dexterous heave and toss, had wrought a somerset upon the Indian; so that with the next trial, he came forth in the good old way —head foremost. As for the great head itself, that was doing as well as could be expected."

As a boy, Carl went through a period of monumental hay fever marked by no ordinary sneezes, but by explosions, one following another in rapid succession so that they seemed continuous, his eyes, nose and mouth became fountains. I see him now as I came upon him one day, where he had gone to isolate himself during an attack, in an unused room of the house. Glancing at me, through bloodshot, aqueous eyes, he turned, in sequence, to the four points of the compass, saluting each with a shattering blast that doubled him over, scattered spray to the walls, and brought his forehead nearly to his feet. Subsiding a moment, shoulders and head hanging to one side, he turned to me and spoke, the words running together in his wet mouth:

"I must have the ocean in my head."

And there were allusions, legendary in the family—to a difficulty immediately following his birth. The doctor diagnosed <u>Hydrocephalus Internus</u>:

> "In <u>infants</u>, the most notable symptom is the progressive enlargement of the head. The fontanels remain open and are tense, and often the sagittal suture fails to close . . . The bones of the skull are thin. The face of the child appears small because of the cranial enlargement and the bulging overhanging forehead. The hair is thin. The skin appears to be tightly stretched and the veins are prominent. The thin orbital plates are pushed downward, with displacement of the eyeballs, so that each iris and often a part of the pupil is covered by the lower lid, and the sclera is visible above. Optic neuritis, followed by optic atrophy, results from pressure of the distended third ventricle upon the chiasm. Strabismus is usually present. The child's head has a tendency to fall backward or to one side, and cannot be held erect. The extremities and trunk are thin and there is rigidity, especially of the abductor muscles. Late in the disease there is spasticity. Convulsions are caused by pressure on the cortex. If the child walks at all, it is with difficulty. Mental development is usually arrested and varying degrees of mental deficiency result, depending upon the amount of ventricular distortion and the severity of the pressure."

But the condition disappeared, as mysteriously as it had arrived, and the doctor could only assume that there had been a rupture or absorption of adhesions. This was the beginning—the headwaters, perhaps— of a series of unique medical phenomena that occurred throughout Carl's generally robust life.

Shifting in the chair, I get to my feet, stand up, and look down at the row of books: the medical books. I think again of my diploma, unframed, and of the back-breaking burden of dollars and hope—my own and my parents'—invested in my education. There is the sound of television and children from downstairs. Sitting again, leaning on my elbows, I recall a visit to a hospital ward, when the doctor, knowing me for a medical student, pointed out a crippled youth, and asked me, half-facetiously, what I would do for him:

> there was the face, the
> white-blue face, and the body,
> the young man, band leader,
> he had sleep-walked out a
> second-story window to be found
>
> legs paralyzed
> from the hips down,
> hands stove,
>
> and the eyes, the
> pale blue watery
> eyes . . .
>
> they sent him home, and
> he lives now, on a narrow board
> of a bed, day and night,
> smoking,
>
> attended by a mother who
> shuts the door . . .

What would I do:

> to bring back,
> to save,
> to return,
>
> a not very talented musician . . .

And there is Melville, in White-Jacket:

> *"Strange! that so many of those who would fain minister to our own health should look so much like invalids themselves."*

And Carl, reading Melville:

> *"In the case of a Sperm Whale the brains are accounted a fine dish. The casket of the skull is broken into with an axe, and the two plump, whitish lobes being withdrawn (precisely resembling two large puddings), they are then mixed with flour, and cooked into a most delectable mess . . ."*

And, again, the way he held the book, possessing it, as though the open halves of it were themselves two plump, whitish lobes . . . he smiled broadly, smacking his lips.

Letting my eyes close, and my arms hang over the sides of the chair—I experience motion once more,

not this time as the house pitching, the stocks dragging, but as a thing, familiar, expected; as a man might climb into his berth before his ship is under way, and then the motion, the departure, the gentle slipping away from the wharf, comes as a thing good and confirming.

Melville, regarding <u>Mardi</u>, in a letter:

> ". . . *proceeding in my narrative of facts, I began to feel an incurable distaste for the same; & a longing to plume my powers for a flight, & felt irked, cramped & fettered by plodding along with dull commonplaces,—So suddenly abandoning the thing altogether, I went to work heart & soul at a romance which is now in fair progress . . .*"

The illusion I have is of being split from head to toe, as in hemiplegia or an imperfect twinning process—with separate circulation on each side, the blood rushing furiously. There are no recalls, no flashing images, no digging in and rooting of the body—rather, the beginning of a journey such as I have never before taken

GENOA

ONE

THERE was the man from Genoa, who went to sea at fourteen, and

> "I have been twenty-three years upon the sea without quitting it for any time long enough to be counted, and I saw all the East and West . . ."

A Man

> ". . . of a good size and looks, taller than the average and of sturdy limbs; the eyes lively and the other features of the face in good proportion; the hair very red; and the complexion somewhat flushed and freckled; a good speaker, cautious and of great talent and an elegant latinist and a most learned cosmographer, graceful when he wished, irate when he was crossed . . .":

Christopher Columbus.

The wind rises again, sifting through the cracks at the eaves, and I draw close to the old chimney. My head seems large, and my legs feel as though joined, wedge-shaped. I read

that twenty-five thousand years ago Cro-Magnon man invaded Europe, from unknown origins. He was tall, averaging above six feet, and had a large brain case, larger than any known man of the present. Settling in southern France, he pushed over the mountains, to the Spanish Peninsula. He worshipped bulls, and buried his dead facing west,

the direction in which he migrated, moving, perhaps, all the way to the brink, the eaves of the unknown ocean, to Cabo de São Vicente, which Columbus called "the beginning of Europe."

Eastward on the map, there is Genoa, at the northernmost pitch of the Ligurian Sea, with land and water falling away southwestward,

just as, beyond Gibralter, beyond the Pillars of Hercules, from Palos the ocean falls away from the land, again southwestward,

and further eastward, there is Crete, progenitor of Greece . . . but

> "'A man overboard!' I shouted at the top of my compass; and like lightning the cords slid through our blistering hands, and with a tremendous shock the boat bounded on the sea's back. One mad sheer and plunge, one terrible strain on the tackles as we sunk in the trough of the waves, tugged upon by the towing breaker, and our knives severed the tackle ropes—we hazarded not unhooking the blocks—our oars were out, and the good boat headed round, with prow to leeward."

Melville in Mardi, with Jarl the Viking, stole a whaleboat and escaped the Arcturian—" . . . and right into the darkness, and dead to leeward, we rowed and sailed . . ."

As earlier, with Toby, he had in fact jumped ship to the valley of the Typee, he now, in the same south seas, with northman as companion, fictively jumped ship into open waters, and

> " . . . West, West! Whitherward point Hope and prophet-fingers; whitherward, at sunset, kneel all worshipers of fire; whitherward in mid-ocean, the great whales turn to die . . ."

sailed westward to fabulous Mardi

> (to be greeted as a white god from the east, as Columbus and his men were greeted in the Indies . . .

Melville, out of the known cosmos of the sperm whaler, leaped to the unknown . . .

> " . . . I've chartless voyaged. With compass and the lead, we had not found these Mardian Isles. Those who boldly launch, cast off all cables; and turning from the common breeze, that's fair for all, with their own breath, fill their own sails. Hug the shore, naught

36

new is seen; and 'Land ho!' at last was sung, when a new world was sought.

"But this new world here sought, is stranger far than his, who stretched his vans from Palos. It is the world of mind; wherein the wanderer may gaze round with more of wonder . . ."

To guarantee escape—a thousand miles at sea in an open boat were not enough—Melville cut off the father ship, the whaler from which he fled,

"For of the stout Arcturian no word was ever heard, from the dark hour we pushed from her fated planks."

and thus made of himself an Ishmael—wanderer in space.

But for Melville, space and time are one . . .

"Do you believe that you lived three thousand years ago? That you were at the taking of Tyre, were overwhelmed in Gomorrah? No. But for me, I was at the subsiding of the Deluge, and helped swab the ground, and build the first house. With the Israelites, I fainted in the wilderness; was in court, when Solomon outdid all the judges before him. I, it was, who . . . touched Isabella's heart, that she hearkened to Columbus."

I become aware now of a different sensation, and realize that it has been with me for some moments:

It is the sound of silence. Wind and rain have vanished, child and home noises from below are hushed. I have fallen into a void, have journeyed to beginnings earlier than I have yet discovered. I sit still, clamoring for a sound; my head feels huge, my body and legs are one.

"If therefore," as Einstein says, "a body is removed sufficiently far from all other masses of the universe its inertia must be reduced to zero."

And Bondi: "This in turn implies that it is possible to introduce an omnipresent cosmic time which has the property of measuring proper time . . ."

And further: "A separate time-reckoning belongs therefore to every natural phenomenon."

"The picture of the history of the universe . . . , then, was that for an infinite period in the distant past there was a completely

37

homogeneous distribution of matter in equilibrium . . . until some event started off the expansion, which has been going on at an increasing pace ever since."

Stubb, in Moby-Dick: "I wonder, Flask, whether the world is anchored anywhere; if she is, she swings with an uncommon long cable . . ."

And Melville, in a letter: ". . . & for me, I shall write such things as the Great Publisher of Mankind ordained ages before he published 'The World'—this planet, I mean . . ."

Again, in Moby-Dick: "When I stand among these mighty Leviathan skeletons . . . I am, by a flood, borne back to that wondrous period, ere time itself can be said to have begun; for time began with man. Here Saturn's gray chaos rolls over me, and I obtain dim, shuddering glimpses into those Polar eternities; when wedged bastions of ice pressed hard upon what are now the Tropics; and in all the 25,000 miles of this world's circumference, not an inhabitable hand's breadth of land was visible."

Rousing, shifting myself, I feel impelled to break through the silence. I find it an effort, muscular, involving sensation at once stiff and pliant in the inner ear, down the sides of the neck, and in the shoulders; and it is not until I rise to my feet and tap my fingers sharply on the desk, that I realize the silence has been altogether subjective—wind and rain have not ceased, the children are still below; I have been controlling these sounds, turning the volume down, as in functional deafness. Experimenting, I realize that the volume is still down, that I wish it to be that way. For an instant, hope and excitement flash through me, so that, in this moment, my two feet are equivalent and normal. This passes quickly. I sink into the chair, and the old sensations of deformity, actual and projected, overtake me, in the silence. I am at once clubfooted and footless.

Melville, describing a calm: "At first he is taken by surprise, never having dreamt of a state of existence where existence itself seems suspended. He shakes himself in his coat, to see whether it be empty or no. He closes his eyes, to test the reality of the glassy expanse. He fetches a deep breath, by way of experiment, and for the sake of witnessing the effect."

"The stillness of the calm is awful. His voice begins to grow

*strange and portentous. He feels it in him like something
swallowed too big for the esophagus. It keeps up a sort of in-
voluntary interior humming in him, like a live beetle. His
cranium is a dome full of reverberations. The hollows of his very
bones are as whispering galleries. He is afraid to speak loud, lest
he be stunned . . ."*

*"But that morning, the two gray firmaments of sky and water
seemed collapsed into a vague ellipsis . . . Every thing was fused
into the calm: sky, air, water, and all. Not a fish was to be seen.
The silence was that of a vacuum. No vitality lurked in the air.
And this inert blending and brooding of all things seemed gray
chaos in conception."*

*And there is Ahab, in <u>Moby-Dick</u>: ". . . not the smallest atom
stirs or lives on matter, but has its cunning duplicate in mind."*

An odor—the odor of sulphur—comes to me. I turn my head vari-
ously, but the odor persists. Powerful, sourceless, it pervades the attic.
I reach for the medical book, and read

that at one time there was a popular theory, disproved in 1668, that slime and
decaying matter were capable of giving rise to living animals, and

that the human spermatozoön was discovered by Leeuwenhoek in 1677 . . .

It was believed, according to the theory of preformation, that fully formed human
bodies existed in miniature in either the sperm or the ovum; all future generations
were thought to be encased, one inside the sex cells of the other, and it was calcu-
lated that the egg of Eve must have contained two hundred thousand million
human beings, concentrically arranged, and that when all these miniatures were
released and unfolded, the human race would terminate.

> (There is the drawing (Hartsoeker, 1694) of a tiny
> human organism, crouched over, huge-headed,
> encased in a sperm cell. A dark star, four-pointed
> like a compass, covers his pate . . .

And there are the other drawings:

> The testicle, the ovary, the
> head of the sperm, in the
> shape of an egg . . .
>
> the uterus pear-shaped, the ovum,
> round, like a planet . . .
>
> the egg, the pear,
> the planet,

with the flagellum for energy . . .

Glancing at the picture: "Human spermatozoön. Diagrammatic."

and the text: "The head is oval or elliptical, but flattened, so that when viewed in profile it is pear-shaped."

I am aware again of internal sensation, and there is a sudden identification:

"The human spermatozoön possesses a head, a neck, a connecting piece or body, and a tail."

It is this—the huge-headed and long-tailed sensation—that I have been experiencing for some time. Pliant as a creature out of myth, I am—nerve, blood and muscle—disciplined and reshapen. My head is black, the skull-bones inflated, retaining their thickness, but become enormous, cavernous, so that all of me is within the head, only the tail remaining outside: flagellant, spring-like . . .

Again there is motion, this time with awe and terror; for whatever my condition, the condition of thought and flesh, the reality in which I am formed and deformed, in which I am known to myself and to others—all is become mutable. I am monstrous, my head merges into the attic, the attic into blackness . . .

my breath comes rapidly, I am restless . . . flashing the pages before me, I stop at

the picture of the uterus and tubes—like the head of a longhorn steer, the ends of the horns exfoliating with fimbriae,

and the ovum, bursting from the follicle, to become momentarily free in the abdomen, out of all direct contact . . . communicating its condition, perhaps, by means of hormones, but nonetheless adrift, as in an open ocean . . .

Moby-Dick: "*All the yard-arms were tipped with a pallid fire; and touched at each tri-pointed lightning-rod-end with three tapering white flames, each of the three tall masts was silently burning in that sulphurous air . . .*"

And Columbus, reported by Fernando: "On the same Saturday, in the night, was seen St. Elmo, with seven lighted tapers, at the top-mast. There was much rain and thunder. I mean to say that those lights were seen, which mariners affirm to be the body of St. Elmo, in beholding which they chaunted many litanies and orisons . . ."

The corpusants.

I am still for some moments, as though waiting for lightning—but there is none; only the steady hum of wind and rain, the muffled voices of children, vague sounds of the city in the distance—and the creaking of the television aerial, in the wind, straining the chimney brackets.

In Lisbon,—rank with bodega, wine in the wood, salt fish, tar, tallow, musk and cinnamon—the sailors talk

of monsters in the western ocean, of gorgons and demons, succubi and succubae, maleficent spirits and unclean devils, unspeakable things that command the ocean currents—of cuttlefish and sea serpents, of lobsters the tips of whose claws are fathoms asunder, of sirens and bishop-fish, the Margyzr and Marmennil of the north, goblins who visit the ship at night, singe hair, tie knots in ropes, tear sails to shreds—of witches who raise tempests and gigantic water-spouts that suck ships into the sky—of dragon, crocodile, griffin, hippogrif, Cerberus and Ammit

or Melville:

> *"Megalosaurus, iguanodon,*
> *Palaeotherium glypthaecon,*
> *A Barnum-show raree;*
> *The vomit of slimy and sludgey sea:*
> *Purposeless creatures, odd inchoate things*
> *Which splashed thro' morasses on fleshly*
> *wings;*
> *The cubs of Chaos, with eyes askance,*
> *Preposterous griffins that squint at Chance*
> *. . ."*

And the medical book:

> "At one time the human sperm cells were regarded as parasites, and under this misapprehension the name spermatozoa, or 'semen animals,' was given to them."

Melville again:

> *"You must have plenty of sea-room to tell the Truth in; especially*
> *when it seems to have an aspect of newness, as America did in*
> *1492, though it was then just as old, and perhaps older than*
> *Asia, only those sagacious philosophers, the common sailors,*

had never seen it before, swearing it was all water and moon-
shine there."

The sailors talked of islands:

of Antilia, and the splendid mirages beyond Gomera; of the French
and Portuguese Green Island, and the Irish O'Brasil;

of the great pines, of a kind unknown, cast ashore on the Azores by
west and north-west winds—and the lemons, green branches and other
fruits washing upon the Canaries;

of Saint Brandon's, to be seen now and again from the Canaries, but
always eluding discovery,

except by the Saint himself, who set out in search of islands possessing
the delights of paradise, and finally landed,

found a dead giant in a sepulchre, revived him, conversed with him,
found him docile, converted him, and permitted him to die again.

The sailors talked of

"the desert islands inhabited by wild men with tails . . ."

or of Atlantis, where the gods were born, and whose first king, Uranus, was given
to prophecy . . .

discovered, perhaps, by Phoenicians blown west, and reported by Silenus (whose
words are beyond question, as he was drunk at the time) to be "a mass of dry land,
which in greatness was infinite and immeasurable, and it nourishes and maintains
by virtue of its green meadow and pastures many great and mighty beasts. The
men who inhabit this clime are more than twice the height of human stature . . ."

The shore was lofty and precipitous, with a vast, fertile plain lying inland, and
great mountains to the north. The land abounded in all precious minerals, and
cattle and elephants were plentiful.

> (modern excavations in southwest Spain have un-
> earthed elephant tusks . . .

There was a canal, and a proud, barbaric city, with copper-clad walls, and a great
temple to Poseidon, clad with silver, and a gigantic statue in gold.

And there was Scheria, home of Nausicaa and the Phaeacians, Ulysses' longest
resting place before his return home—like Atlantis, it boasted a great city, and
was located beyond the Pillars of Hercules.

And Tarshish, the port for which Jonah set sail from Joppa.

> *(Melville in Joppa: "No sleep last night—*

only resource to cut tobacco, and watch the
six windows of my room, which is like a
lighthouse— & hear the surf & wind . . . I
have such a feeling in this lonely old Joppa,
with the prospect of a long detention here,
owing to the surf—that it is only by stern
self-control & grim defiance that I continue
to keep cool and patient."

Joppa, the point of departure, the Palos, from which Jonah sought to escape, to Tarshish . . .

But perhaps Tarshish, Atlantis and Scheria were all one: islands, locked in the minds of those who dwelt in the internal sea . . .

perhaps they were all Cadiz: the barbaric western city beyond the Pillars, on the southwest shore of Spain (not far from Palos), where the Guadalquivir pours into "the real ocean," as the Egyptian priest called it; or, in the words of the Arabians, "the green sea of gloom" . . .

The Western Ocean.

**In Lisbon, the sailors say: "He who sails beyond the Cape of
No may return or not.**

**"For many said: how is it possible to sail beyond a Cape which
the navigators of Spain had set as the terminus and end of all
navigation in those parts, as men who knew that the sea beyond was not navigable, not only because of the strong currents, but because it was very broken with so much boiling
over of its waters that it sucked up all the ships."**

T W O

there was Marco Polo, talking of Cipango, from a jail cell in Genoa:

reporting it to be fifteen hundred miles east of Asia, to be reached by huge Chinese ships made of the fir tree, ships that sailed freely upon the ocean that washed the eastern shores of that continent . . .

(and if Asia extended to the ocean, and

Cipango were fifteen hundred miles east
of Asia—to where did the ocean extend?

*And Melville in Genoa: "Ramparts overhanging the open sea,
arches thrown over ravines. Fine views of sections of town. Up &
up. Galley-slave prison. Gratings commanding view of sea—
infinite liberty."*

And Genoa itself:

*"Janus, the first king of Italy, and descended from the Giants,
founded Genoa on this spot in the time of Abraham; and Janus,
Prince of Troy, skilled in astronomy, while sailing in search of a
place wherein to dwell in healthfulness and security, came to the
same Genoa founded by Janus, King of Italy and great-grandson
of Noah; and seeing that the sea and the encompassing hills
seemed in all things convenient, he increased it in fame and
greatness."*

Janus, Roman god,

doorkeeper of the firmament, presider over gates, the entrance upon
and beginning of things . . .

Ianus geminus, faced front and back,

East and West . . .

I close my eyes, and there is again a sense of split, a jagged crease
running the length of my forehead—only for a moment, and it is gone.

Genoa,

at the northernmost pitch of the Ligurian Sea, turning

southeast, to trade with the East, and

southwest, perhaps, through the Pillars of Hercules, to

the Terrestrial Paradise . . . (for many philosophers believe this will be
found south of the equator, the torrid zone serving as a flaming sword
to ward off invasion. They divide the globe into northern and southern
hemispheres, the southern being the head, or better part, and the
northern the feet, or lesser part (this being confirmed by the stars of
the southern hemisphere, which shine with a larger and brighter aspect). The east, according to the philosophers, is to the right, and to
the left, the west.)

In Genoa, in the year 1451, Susanna Columbus, wife to Domenico, gave birth to a son, Christopher . . .

> **"His parents were notable persons, one time rich . . . ; at other times they must have been poor . . ."**

> *Allan Melvill, Herman's father, in a letter: "I have now to request in the most* <u>urgent manner</u>*, as equally involving my personal honor & the welfare of my Family, that you would favor me by* <u>return of mail</u> *with your Note to my Order at six months from 31st March, for Five Thousand Dollars . . ."*

At the age of fourteen, Columbus went to sea . . .

> *Melville: "Sad disappointments in several plans which I had sketched for my future life; the necessity of doing something for myself, united to a naturally roving disposition, had now conspired within me, to send me to sea as a sailor."*

and

> *". . . thought me an erring and a wilful boy, and perhaps I was; but if I was, it had been a hard-hearted world and hard times that had made me so. I had learned to think much and bitterly before my time . . ."*

Domenico, Christopher's father, was a well-liked man, easily obtaining property on credit . . .

> *Allan Melvill: "I rec^d this morning with unutterable satisfaction your most opportune & highly esteemed favour . . . with the annexed two notes drawn by yourself . . . one for $2500—the other for $2750—payable at the Bank of America . . ."*

But—a weaver by trade—he neglected his loom, took on sidelines: cheese, wine, a tavern . . . so that Christopher, returning from a sea voyage, age nineteen, found himself responsible for his father's debts, and, with his mariner's wages, secured the father's freedom from a Genoese jail.

> *Allan Melvill: ". . . my situation has become almost intolerable for the want of $500 to discharge some urgent debts, and provide necessaries for my Family . . . I may soon be prosecuted for my last quarters Rent, & other demands which were unavoidably left unpaid . . ."*

**Christopher remained, throughout his life, mysterious regarding his
origins, speaking of himself never as Genoese, but only as foreigner...**

*Ahab, gazing at the corpusants: "Oh, thou magnanimous! Now I
do glory in my genealogy! ... thou foundling fire, thou hermit
immemorial, thou too hast thy incommunicable riddle, thy un-
participated grief. Here again with haughty agony, I read my
sire."*

Columbus and Melville—the paternity blasted ...

(perhaps Domenico and Allan should have
practised a custom of the Iberians and
Caribs,

(The Couvade,

(the father taking to his bed for several
days or weeks at the birth of a child, so as
not to endanger the delicate affinity with
the newborn ...

Columbus:

**"Most exalted Sovereigns: At a very early age I entered upon
the sea navigating, and I have continued doing so until today.
The calling in itself inclines whoever follows it to desire to
know the secrets of this world. Forty years are already passing
which I have employed in this manner: I have traversed every
region which up to the present time is navigated."**

**"During this time I have seen, and in seeing, have studied
all writings, cosmography, histories, chronicles, and philosophy and those relating to other arts, by means of which our
Lord made me understand with a palpable hand, that it was
practicable to navigate from here to the Indies and inspired
me with a will for the execution of this navigation. And with
this fire, I came to your Highnesses."**

*Melville, as Pierre: "A varied scope of reading, little suspected
by his friends, and randomly acquired by a random but lynx-
eyed mind ...; this poured one considerable contributory stream
into that bottomless spring of original thought which the occasion
and time had caused to burst out in himself."*

Columbus:

"It might be that your Highnesses and all the others who knew me, . . . either in secret or public would reprove me in divers manners, saying that I am not learned in letters and calling me a crazy sailor, a worldly man, etc."

"I say that the holy spirit works in Christians, Jews, Moors, and in all others of all sects, and not only in the wise but the ignorant: for in my time I have seen a villager who gave a better account of the heaven and the stars and their courses than others who expended money in learning of them."

And Melville—always a man of the fo'castle:

"*. . . a whale-ship was my Yale College and my Harvard.*"

Christopher, who called himself "an ignorant man," was captain of his own ship and a corsair, at twenty-one. And

". . . I saw all the East and West . . ."

Once,

"It happened to me that King Reynal . . . sent me to Tunis to seize the galleas Fernandina, and when I was already on the island of St. Peter in Sardinia, a settee informed me that the galleas was accompanied by two other ships and a carack, whereupon there was agitation among the men and they refused to sail on unless we returned first to Marseilles to pick up another ship and more men. Seeing that I could not force their hand without some artifice, I agreed to what they asked me, but, changing the bait of the magnetic needle, I spread sails at sunset, and the next morning, at dawn, we were within the cape of Carthagine while all had been certain that we were going to Marseilles."

Moby-Dick: "Thrusting his head halfway into the binnacle, Ahab caught one glimpse of the compasses; his uplifted arm slowly fell; for a moment he almost seemed to stagger. Standing behind him Starbuck looked, and lo! the two compasses pointed East, and the 'Pequod' was as infallibly going West."

Fourteen hundred seventy-eight and -nine: Columbus in all probability sailed to the East, in the service of the House of Centurione. The course was through the Straits of Messina,

(Melville: "*Coasts of Calabria & Sicily*

47

ahead at day break. Neared them at 10
o'clock ... At 1 P.M. anchored in harbor of
Messina ... Rainy day.")

... thence across the Ionian Sea to Taenarum, through the Cervi
Channel north of Cythera, past the white columns of the Temple of
Poseidon on Cape Sunium, through the difficult currents of the
D'Oro channel to Cape Mastika and the island of Chios, due south
of Lesbos.

> Melville: "*Sea less cross. At 12.M. pleasant, & made the coast of*
> *Greece, the Morea. Passed through the straits, & Cape Matapan.*"

Matapan being the Taenarum of Christopher ...

Thus Columbus before the Indies, and Melville, after Polynesia ...
rubbing among the old islands ...

And August the thirteenth, 1476, Columbus, on board a Genoese
trading vessel, engaged in sea-battle with a Franco-Portuguese out-
fit: another ship locked with his, both caught fire, and both eventually
went down. Columbus, in the open sea,

> (*Melville: "A bloody film was before my*
> *eyes, through which, ghost-like, passed and*
> *repassed my father, mother, and sisters. An*
> *unutterable nausea oppressed me; I was*
> *conscious of gasping; there seemed no breath*
> *in my body ... I thought to myself, Great*
> *God! this is death!*"

... grasped an oar and, alternately swimming and resting, despite
wounds, finally landed at Lagos, twenty miles from "the beginning of
Europe," and not far from Cadiz and Palos.

> de Madariaga: "On August 13th, 1476, Christoforo Columbo,
> then just under twenty-five years of age, was in danger of
> death. He was near enough to death to be able to say that on
> that day he was reborn."

> Melville, to Hawthorne: "*My development has been all within a*
> *few years past. I am like one of those seeds taken out of the*
> *Egyptian Pyramids, which, after being three thousand years a*
> *seed & nothing but a seed, being planted in English soil, it de-*

*veloped itself, grew to greenness, and then fell to mould. So I.
Until I was twenty-five, I had no development at all. From my
twenty-fifth year I date my life."*

I shift my position, turn to sit sideways, throwing one leg over the arm
of the chair. The strange internal sensations are still with me, but are
less terrifying, with greater possibility of change . . .

**In Portugal, Columbus, Genoese Ishmael, married one Filipa Moniz
Perestrello, of an old, established family, and thus took a step up the
ladder, toward the court,**

as Herman married, or was married perhaps, to Lizzie Shaw . . .

> "Not the slightest hint has come down to us of the appear-
> ance or disposition of Columbus's only wife; Dona Felipa is
> as shadowy a figure as the Discoverer's mother."

But there was Beatriz,

**whom he loved and did not marry . . . whose last name, despite all
attempts by herself and family to suppress it, was Torquemada, and
whose origin, therefore, was probably Jewish . . .**

**Christopher and Beatriz—joined, not in matrimony, but in blasted
paternity—got a son, the illegitimate Ferdinand (who later claimed
noble ancestry for his father),**

*as, in Pierre, Mr. Glendinning begat upon his French mistress a daugh-
ter, Isabel,*

> (and perhaps, in Polynesia, Herman and
> Fayaway . . .

**But in Portugal, with the help of Dona Felipa, Columbus gained the
court:**

> "The King, as he observed this <u>Christovao Colom</u> to be a big
> talker and boastful in setting forth his accomplishments,
> and full of fancy and imagination with his Isle Cypango than
> certain whereof he spoke, gave him small credit. However, by
> strength of his importunity it was ordered that he confer
> with D. Diego Ortiz bishop of Ceuta and Master Roderigo and
> Master José, to whom the King had committed these matters
> of cosmography and discovery, and they all considered the

words of <u>Christovao Colom</u> as vain, simply founded on imagination, or things like that Isle Cypango of Marco Polo . . ."

And so he left the court, left Portugal, left Dona Felipa . . .

became, in fact, the ideal unwed Ishmael, wanderer in the wilderness, of which Melville, long since returned from the seas, never stopped thinking . . .

> *(Pasted to the inside of Melville's desk, dis-*
> *covered after his death: "Keep true to the*
> *dreams of thy youth."*

Christopher, wed "to the magnanimity of the sea, which" as Melville says, "will permit no records" . . .

searching an insular paternity, left Portugal, for Spain

T H R E E

and Isabella,

who, like himself, was blue-eyed, fair-skinned and red-haired . . .

He told her, perhaps, of the books he had been reading, such as the <u>Ymago Mundi</u>:

> "There is a spring in Paradise which waters the Garden of
> Delights and which splays into four rivers."
> "The Paradise on Earth is a pleasant place, situated in
> certain regions of the Orient, at a long distance by land and
> by sea from our inherited world. It rises so high that it
> touches the lunar sphere . . ."

> *(Melville, <u>Billy Budd</u>: "Who in the rainbow*
> *can draw the line where the violet tint ends*
> *and the orange tint begins? Distinctly we*
> *see the difference of the color, but where ex-*
> *actly does the first one visibly enter into the*
> *other? So with sanity and insanity."*

"... and the water of the Deluge could not reach it... its altitude over the lowlands is incomparable ... and it reaches the layers of calm air which lie on top of the zone of troubled air ..."

"From this lake, as from a main spring, there flow the four rivers of Paradise: Phison or Ganges; Gihon or Nile; Tigris and Euphrates ..."

Certain it is that Melville performed an act original and radical to himself, in Moby-Dick. In all his works hitherto, he had voyaged southward to Cape Horn, then westward to the Pacific, returning via that same essentially western route (the one exception being Redburn, dealing not at all with the Pacific, nor with cosmographical man).

"... the sight of many unclad, lovely island creatures, round the Horn"—that was the route to the Treasures: southward, the Horn, and then west.

But in Moby-Dick, Melville turned upon himself and Western Man, performing an act as violent as subsequent war and catastrophe—an act rich, perhaps, with revenge as Ahab's pursuit of the whale: the Pequod turned and headed back east—a route Melville himself never followed to the Pacific—eastward, via Good Hope, the Indian Ocean, and

"By the straits of Sunda, chiefly, vessels bound to China from the west, emerge into the China seas."

Thus, it was a return, a going back, a going back upward, perhaps...

like the Pacific salmon, who spend their lives in salt water, and then, anadromous, run upward to the fresh, to the very individual source waters, the headwaters, to spawn and die

(developing, often, a hump back, hooked snout and elongated jaw—becoming altogether monstrous, while in this pursuit
. . .

Columbus: "I always read that the world, land and water, was spherical ... Now I observed so much divergence, that I began to hold different views about the world and I found that it was not round ... but pear-shaped, round except where it has a nipple, for there it is taller, or as if one had a round ball and, on one side, it should be like a woman's breast, and this nipple part is the highest and closest to heaven . . ."

Columbus, ascending the mounting waters, "running upward" to the very source point, "highest and closest to heaven" . . .

> *Genesis, the St. Jerome version: "But the Lord God in the beginning had planted a Paradise of Delight: in which he placed the man whom he had fashioned . . . And a river came out from the Place of Delight to water Paradise: which from thence is divided into four heads . . ."*

Spanish cosmographers, however, were not impressed. In fourteen hundred ninety, they "judged his promises and offers were impossible and vain and worthy of rejection . . . they ridiculed his reasoning saying that they had tried so many times and had sent ships in search of the mainland and that it was all air and there was no reason in it . . ."

> *Lizzie Melville, Herman's wife, in a letter to her mother: "I suppose by this time you are deep in the 'fogs' of 'Mardi'—if the mist ever does clear away, I should like to know what it reveals . . ."*

They further advised the Sovereigns "that it was not a proper object for their royal authority to favor an affair that rested on such weak foundations, and which appeared uncertain and impossible to any educated person, however little learning he might have."

But Columbus "had conceived in his heart the most certain confidence to find what he claimed he would, as if he had this world locked up in his trunk."

> Later, in the Indies:
> "We reached the latter island near a large mountain which seemed almost to reach heaven, and in the centre of that mountain there was a peak which was much higher than all the rest of the mountain, and from which many streams flowed in different directions, especially toward the direction in which we lay. At a distance of three leagues a waterfall appeared as large through as an ox, which precipitated itself from such a high point that it seemed to fall from heaven. It was at such a distance that there were many wagers on the

ships, as some said that it was white rocks and others that it was water. As soon as they arrived nearer, the truth was learned, and it was the most wonderful thing in the world to see from what a high place it was precipitated and from what a small place such a large waterfall sprang."

And the Pequod, approaching the Straits of Sunda:

"Broad on both bows, at the distance of some two or three miles, and forming a great semi-circle, embracing one half of the level horizon, a continuous chain of whale-jets were up-playing and sparkling in the noonday air."

Swinging my foot to the floor, I sit tense, crouched forward, straight in the chair. Huge-headed, I am one of millions, and there is a gateway, an opening, for which all of us have been alerted.

"As marching armies approaching an unfriendly defile in the mountains, accelerate their march, all eagerness to place that perilous passage in their rear, and once more expand in comparative security upon the plain; even so did this vast fleet of whales now seem hurrying forward through the straits; gradually contracting the wings of their semicircle, and swimming on, in one solid, but still crescentic centre."

From Nantucket, east,

to Good Hope, the Indian Ocean, the Straits of Sunda, and

". . . we glided between two whales into the innermost heart of the shoal, as if from some mountain torrent we had slid into a serene valley lake. Here the storms in the roaring glens between the outermost whales, were heard but not felt. In this central expanse the sea presented the smooth satin-like surface, called a sleek, produced by the subtle moisture thrown off by the whale in his more quiet moods. Yes, we were now in that enchanted calm which they say lurks at the heart of every commotion."

"Keeping at the centre of the lake, we were occasionally visited by small tame cows and calves; the women and children of this routed host."

"Some of the subtlest secrets of the seas seemed divulged to us in this enchanted pond. We saw young Leviathan amours in the deep."

53

And Columbus, on the third voyage, sailing in the Gulf of Paria, observing the mangroves lining the shore, with tiny oysters clinging to their roots ... the oyster shells open, to catch from the mangrove leaves the dewdrops that engender pearls ...

Fourteen hundred and ninety, Isabella, rejecting the advice of her cosmographers, was hesitant. Perhaps, with insanity touching her mother and her daughter, rendering her thus bracketed

> (as Melville, his father dying maniacal and
> his son a suicide, was similarly bracketed),

she was just strange enough to listen ...

Certainly, the natural direction for Spain's colonial expansion was Africa, in pursuit of the Moors. America was altogether irrelevant, distant, difficult, tempting, and ultimately untenable and ruinous. Thus, as Melville to Western Man, so Columbus to Spanish history, did more violence, perhaps, than all the wars that followed.

But as Albertus Magnus said of the Antipodes:

> *"Perhaps also some magnetic power in that region draws human*
> *stones even as the magnet draws iron."*

F O U R

And there was Michele de Cuneo, with his Carib slave: "Having taken her into my cabin, she being naked according to their custom, I conceived a desire to take pleasure. I wanted to put my desire into execution but she did not want it and treated me with her fingernails in such manner that I wished I had never begun. But seeing that (to tell you the end of it all), I took a rope and thrashed her well, for which she raised such unheard of screams that you would not have believed your ears. Finally we came to an agreement in such a manner that I can tell you that she seemed to have been brought up in a school of harlots."

And the letter to the Marquis of Mantua, announcing that

vessels of the King of Spain "discovered certain islands, among others a very large island toward the Orient which had very great rivers and terrible mountains and a most fertile country inhabited by handsome men and women, but they all go naked, except that some wear a leaf of cotton over their genitals . . ."

Melville, in Typee:

". . . we found ourselves close in with the island the next morning, but as the bay we sought lay on its farther side, we were obliged to sail some distance along the shore, catching, as we proceeded, short glimpses of blooming valleys, deep glens, waterfalls, and waving groves, hidden here and there by projecting and rocky headlands, every moment opening to the view some new and startling scene of beauty."

"As they drew nearer, and I watched the rising and sinking of their forms, and beheld the uplifted right arm bearing above the water the girdle of tapa, and their long dark hair trailing beside them as they swam, I almost fancied they could be nothing else than so many mermaids . . ."

(Columbus, First Voyage: "On the previous day, when the Admiral went to the Rio del Oro, he saw three mermaids, which rose well out of the sea . . .")

Typee: "We were still some distance from the beach, and under slow headway, when we sailed right into the midst of these swimming nymphs, and they boarded us at every quarter; many seizing hold of the chainplates and springing into the chains; others . . . wreathing their slender forms about the ropes . . . All of them at length succeeded in getting up the ship's side, where they clung dripping with the brine and glowing from the bath, their jet-black tresses streaming over their shoulders, and half-enveloping their otherwise naked forms. There they hung, sparkling with savage vivacity . . ."

"Our ship was now given up to every species of riot . . ."

But Columbus in Spain, fourteen eighty-five to ninety-two:

"All this delay did not go without great anguish and grief for

Cristóbal Colón, for . . . he saw his life was flowing past wasted . . . , and above all because he saw how distrusted his truth and person were, which for generous persons it is known to be as painful and detestable as death."

Columbus waited.

F I V E

I am lifted from my chair, headlong. I stand, leaning over the desk, my head whirling, consonant with the gusts of blackberry winter, of the catbird storm. Decision crowds upon me, and, like one of the sperm whales crowding for the Straits of Sunda, pursued by a Nantucket madman who is in turn pursued by Malays, I push for a gateway, an entrance upon and beginning of things.

August 2nd, 1492,

ninth day of the Jewish Ab, The Father, when Jewry mourned the destruction of Jerusalem . . . the exodus from Spain began. Three hundred thousand funneled to the seaports, not far from "the beginning of Europe."

> "Those who went to embark in El Puerto de Santa Maria and in Cadiz, as soon as they saw the sea, shouted and yelled, men and women, grown-ups and children, asking mercy of the Lord in their prayers, and they thought they would see some marvels from God and that they would have a road opened for them across the sea . . . ."

But the Jews embarked and headed back east, into the internal sea, to the old haunts . . . and

on that day, Columbus ordered his men aboard three ships, before nightfall.

Perhaps, within himself, Christopher journeyed to the old haunts, herded himself into the tribe, to Esdras of the Apocrypha, to the earlier prophets, and to Genesis;

but it is not so much that Columbus may have been a Jew, or Melville at war with Christ, as it is that both men ran upward to the sources. Melville, an Ishmael, and Columbus, displaying an arrogance greater than Joan's, sought the prophets—men who, like the first king of Atlantis, imagined and predicted, and from whom, therefore, action flowed . . .

> (Columbus the navigator: "All people received their astronomy from the Jews."

August 3,

before daylight of a gray, calm day—a day so quiet that one would think time had stopped—three ships slipped from their moorings— the motion a thing good and confirming—and drifted down the Rio Tinto on the tide. Guided by the sweeps, with no wind, the ships altered their course to port, and entered the Rio Saltes, floating past the piney sand dunes, and spoke another ship, outward bound on the same tide, with a cargo of emigrant Jews

> (and the Pinta spoke the same ship on the return voyage of both, the one bound from the Levant, the other from the Indies . . .

Turning fifty degrees to starboard, the fleet crossed the bar, and

> "proceeded with a strong breeze until sunset, towards the south, for 60 miles, equal to 15 leagues . . ."

There was the letter from Paul Toscanelli, Florentine physician and philosopher (in those days, the one implied the other):

> "To Christopher Columbus, Paul the physician, greeting:
> "I see your great and magnificent desire to go where the spices grow, and in reply to your letter I send you the copy of another letter which I wrote a long time ago . . . and I send you another seaman's chart . . . "
> "And although I know from my own knowledge that the world can be shown as it is in the form of a sphere, I have determined for greater facility and greater intelligence to show the said route by a chart similar to those which are made for navigation . . . straight to the west the commencement of the Indies is shown, and the islands and places where you can deviate towards the equinoctial line, and by how

> much space, that is to say, in how many leagues you can reach those most fertile places, filled with all kinds of spices and jewels and precious stones: and you must not wonder if I call the place where spices grow, <u>West</u>, because it is commonly said that they grow in the <u>East</u>; but whoever will navigate to the West will always find the said places in the West . . ."

But Columbus did not head "straight to the west," but

South and by West, for the Canaries, and, further, for the Terrestrial Paradise . . .

Monday August 6,

> "The rudder of the caravel <u>Pinta</u> became unshipped, and Martin Alonzo Pinzon, who was in command, believed or suspected that it was by contrivance of Gomes Rascon and Cristobal Quintero, to whom the caravel belonged, for they dreaded to go on that voyage. The Admiral says that, before they sailed, these men had been displaying a certain backwardness . . ."

Still standing, I step back from the desk, gaining my sea-legs. I am braced, with one hand on the chimney. The house arches and shudders—an inverted hull, with kelson aloft—against the weather.

and the human sperm enters a reservoir, low in oxygen—and thence to the vas deferens, in the lowest, coolest scrotal area . . .

upward, then, through the spermatic cord, to globus minor and the seminal vesicle . . .

The Canaries: insular remnants, perhaps, of Atlantis—thence to Antillia, showing on Toscanelli's chart half-way to Cathay. Antillia: of which the Indies might be scattered remnants . . .

The ships were shaken down . . . there were no desertions at the Canaries. The voyage was begun . . .

Sunday September 9:

> "On this day they lost sight of land; and many, fearful of not being able to return for a long time to see it, sighed and shed tears. But the admiral . . . when that day the sailors reckoned the distance 18 leagues, said he had counted only 15, having decided to lessen the record so that the crew

would not think they were as far from Spain as in fact they were."

So a great head shrinks the distance . . .

shrinks the very globe itself:—for it was only the bold and persistent acceptance of cosmographical errors in the mind of Columbus—shrinking the earth by a quarter, and juggling Cypango until it fell among the Virgin Islands—that made possible the discovery . . .

> (and in San Salvador, Columbus noted among the natives that "the whole forehead and head is very broad"—the result of artificially flattening the skulls of infants, by pressing them between boards.

Monday September 17:

> **Passing the true north, Columbus—making the "pilot's blessing"—marked the North Star, and noted that the needle now began pointing to the west of north, instead of to the customary east.**

> **"All the sailors feared greatly and all became very sad, and began to murmur under their breaths again, without making it known altogether to Christopher Columbus, seeing such a new thing, and one they had never seen or experienced, and there they feared they were in another world."**

> _Moby-Dick:_—_"At first, the steel went round and round, quivering and vibrating at either end; but at last it settled to its place, when Ahab, who had been intently watching for this result, stepped frankly back from the binnacle, and pointing his stretched arm towards it, exclaimed,—'Look ye, for yourselves, if Ahab be not Lord of the level loadstone! . . .'_
> _"One after another they peered in, for nothing but their own eyes could persuade such ignorance as theirs, and one after another they slunk away."_

Whale, boobie, sandpiper, dove, crab and boatswain bird—all were signs of land . . . for hitherto none had sailed far enough to see such things other than close to land . . .

and there was sargasso weed, rumored to trap ships as in a web . . . detritus, perhaps, of Atlantis . . .

From the posterior, the vault of the vagina, the sperm's journey measures, perhaps, five inches. The cilia in the oviduct have an outward stroke, against the motion of the sperm . . .

> (Columbus reported the usual course of the sargasso weed to be from west to east . . .

In addition, there are the folds and ridges, like waves, of the mucous membrane, and the powerful leukocytes, white monsters that attack the sperm.

> "Forward progress of the human spermatozoön is at the rate of about 1.5 mm a minute which, in relation to their respective lengths, compares well with average swimming ability for man."

Driven by temperature and secretions, the sperm's action is a fight against time; for

> "A spermatozoön is only fertile if it is capable of performing powerful movements."

> **Olson, on Melville: "He only rode his own space once— Moby-Dick. He had to be wild or he was nothing in particular. He had to go fast, like an American . . ."**

Thus, the spermatozoön, like the salmon, swimming "a spiral course upstream."

September 19:

> **". . . but as the land never appeared they presently believed nothing, concluding from those signs since they failed, that they were going through another world whence they would never return."**

September 24:

> **". . . they said that it was a great madness and homicidal on their part, to venture their lives in following out the madness of a foreigner, who . . . had risked his life . . . and was deceiving so many people: especially as his proposition or dream had been contradicted by so many great and lettered men, and considered as vain and foolish: and that it was enough to excuse themselves from whatever might be done in the matter, that they had arrived where men had never dared to navigate, and that they were not obliged to go to the end of the world . . ."**

> **"Some went further, saying, that if he persisted in going onward, that the best thing of all was to throw him into the**

sea some night, publishing that he had fallen in taking the position of the star with his quadrant or astrolabe . . ."

Ahab, in <u>Moby-Dick</u>: "Then gazing at his quadrant, and handling one after the other, its numerous cabalistical contrivances, he pondered again, and muttered: 'Foolish toy! babies' plaything of haughty Admirals, and Commodores, and Captains; the world brags of thee, of thy cunning and might; but what after all canst thou do, but tell the poor, pitiful point, where thou thyself happenest to be in this wide planet, and the hand that holds thee: no! not one jot more! Thou canst not tell where one drop of water or one grain of sand will be to-morrow noon; and yet with thy impotence thou insultest the sun! Science! Curse thee, thou vain toy; and cursed be all things that cast men's eyes aloft to that heaven, whose live vividness but scorches him, as these old eyes are even now scorched with thy light, O sun! Level by nature to this earth's horizon are the glances of man's eyes; not shot from the crown of his head, as if God had meant him to gaze on his firmament. Curse thee, thou quadrant!' dashing it to the deck, 'no longer will I guide my earthly way by thee; the level ship's compass, and the level dead-reckoning, by log and by line; <u>these</u> shall conduct me, and show me my place on the sea.'"

And Columbus—greatest dead-reckoning navigator of all time, whose bearings may be followed and trusted today, whose faulty observations of the stars never interfered with his level look at sea, signs and weather—Columbus

"here says that he has had the quadrant hung up until he reaches land, to repair it . . ."

October 7, course changed from West to West-South-West, to follow the great flocks of birds overhead.

October 10:

"Here the people could endure no longer. They complained of the length of the voyage. But the Admiral cheered them up in the best way he could, giving them good hopes of the advantages they might gain from it. He added that, however much they might complain, he had to go to the Indies, and that he would go on until he found them . . ."

Ahab: "'What is it, what nameless, inscrutable, unearthly thing

61

is it; what cozening, hidden lord and master, and cruel, remorse-less emperor commands me; that against all natural lovings and longings, I so keep pushing, and crowding, and jamming myself on all the time . . .?'"

October 11:

> **The crew of the <u>Pinta</u> picked up "a reed and a stick, and another stick carved, as it seemed, with iron tools and some grass which grows on land and a tablet of wood. They all breathed on seeing these signs and felt great joy."**

October 11:

> **". . . the Admiral asked and admonished the men to keep a good look-out on the forecastle, and to watch well for land . . ."**
>
> *"'It's a white whale, I say' resumed Ahab . . . : 'a white whale. Skin your eyes for him, men; look sharp for white water; if ye see but a bubble, sing out.'"*
>
> **". . . and to him who should first cry out that he saw land, he would give a silk doublet, besides the other rewards promised by the Sovereigns, which were 10,000 maravedis to him who should first see it."**
>
> *"'Whosoever of ye raises me a white-headed whale with a wrinkled brow and a crooked jaw; whosoever of ye raises me that white-headed whale, with three holes punctured in his starboard fluke—look ye, whosoever of ye raises me that same white whale, he shall have this gold ounce my boys!'"*

October 11, course changed again to West.

> (As a traveler to unknown parts, Columbus was of course expected to bring back tales of fish growing on trees, men with tails, and headless people with eyes in their bellies . . .

And there was the light, seen by Columbus—or so he says—two hours before midnight on the Eleventh: ". . . like a little wax candle rising and falling." Be it the pine-knot torch of an Indian . . . sea worms, phosphorescent . . . or the jammed and crowded imaginings of Christopher . . . whatever it be, Columbus, on the strength of it, claimed his own doublet, and the Sovereigns' 10,000 maravedis . . .

Ahab: "'... *the doubloon is mine, Fate reserved the doubloon for me. I only; none of ye could have raised the White Whale first. There she blows! ...*'"

Like a great albuminous globe, monstrous beyond all proportion, the ovum looms ahead . . .

October 12:

"At two hours after midnight the land was sighted . . ."

CHARYBDIS

ONE

AFTER Alaska, Carl came back to Indianapolis, with a duffle bag of old clothes and odd relics . . . bits of bone from walrus, seal and man, pieces of carved wood, various stones shaped by the ocean, or by Carl himself, or perhaps by long-dead Indians. He stayed (as always) only a short time . . . "just long enough to change my sox." Then he was off, apparently without funds (this is another story, where his money came from, where he got it or whose it was—he never seemed to have any except just when he needed it, and then only just enough), heading east . . .

and the next we heard he was in Spain, flying a plane . . . seat of the pants flying, he said, no instruments, no time to learn (he had never flown before) . . . for the Loyalists.

Columbus:

> "This night the wind increased, and the waves were terrible, rising against each other, and so shaking and straining the vessel that she would make no headway, and was in danger of being stove in."

The first return voyage:—as on all eastward voyages, the voyages of return, voyages back—opposite and contrary to those westward—he met dirty weather.

> "At sunrise the wind blew still harder, and the cross sea was terrific. They continued to show the closely-reefed mainsail, to enable her to rise from between the waves, or she would otherwise have been swamped."

For two days, on board the Niña, the officer of the watch scanned each on-coming wave, and gave quick orders to the helmsman, in order that the wave might be met at the best angle. All contact with the

Pinta was lost, and no attempt was made to hold to a course.

"... no one expected to escape, holding themselves for lost, owing to the fearful weather ..."

"Here the Admiral writes of the causes that made him fear he would perish, and of others that gave him hope that God would work his salvation, in order that such news as he was bringing to the Sovereigns might not be lost. It seemed to him the strong desire he felt to bring such great news, and to show that all he had said and offered to discover had turned out true, suggested the fear that he would not be able to do so ..."

(Melville to Hawthorne: "... I am so pulled hither and thither by circumstances. The calm, the coolness, the silent grass-growing mood in which a man ought always to compose,—that, I fear, can seldom be mine."

"He says further that it gave him great sorrow to think of the two sons he had left at their studies in Cordova, who would be left ... without father ..., in a strange land; while the Sovereigns would not know of the services he had performed in this voyage, nor would they receive the prosperous news which would move them to help the orphans."

And Melville in Pittsfield, winter of 1851, writing Moby-Dick: his son Malcolm an infant, and Lizzie pregnant again: to Hawthorne: "Dollars damn me ..."

"... that the Sovereigns might still have information, even if he perished in the storm, he took a parchment and wrote on it as good an account as he could of all he had discovered ... He rolled this parchment up in waxed cloth, fastened it very securely, ordered a large wooden barrel to be brought, and put it inside ... and so he ordered the barrel to be thrown into the sea."

Lizzie, reporting Herman: "Wrote White Whale or Moby Dick under unfavorable circumstances—would sit at his desk all day not eating anything till four or five oclock—then ride to the village after dark ..."

... heading for the conclusion, the disaster, the sinking of the Pequod:

Melville, as Starbuck: "... may survive to hug his wife and child again.—Oh Mary! Mary!—boy! boy! boy! ... who can tell to what unsounded deeps Starbuck's body this day week may sink ...!"

66

And Ahab, to Captain Gardiner of the <u>Rachel</u> (who has begged him to join in searching for his lost son): "Captain Gardiner, I will not do it. Even now I lose time. Good bye, good bye. God bless ye, man, and may I forgive myself . . ."

Ahab to Starbuck: "I see my wife and my child in thine eye."

And: "About this time—yes, it is his noon nap now—the boy vivaciously wakes; sits up in bed; and his mother tells him of me, of cannibal old me . . ."

Pittsfield, 1851—the infant Malcolm; Lizzie, pregnant; and cannibal old Melville, in the chase:

"At length the breathless hunter came so nigh his seemingly unsuspecting prey, that his entire dazzling hump was distinctly visible, sliding along the sea as if an isolated thing, and continually set in a revolving ring of finest, fleecy greenish foam. He saw the vast involved wrinkles of the slightly projecting head beyond."

From the medical book: "It is even assumed that the ovum itself has a certain radiation designed to attract the spermatozoa."

> (*Ahab: ". . . the most vital stuff of vital fathers."*

"As soon as the first spermatozoa have reached the ovum, they surround it and try to penetrate with their heads the outer membrane."

Starbuck: "Oh! my God! what is this that . . . leaves me so deadly calm, yet expectant,—fixed at the top of a shudder! Future things swim before me, as in empty outlines and skeletons; all the past is somehow grown dim. Mary, girl! thou fadest in pale glories behind me; boy! I seem to see but thy eyes grown wondrous blue."

Again, the wind hesitates, the children below are quiet. The sensation I have had of the attic as a ship, pitching upon the plain, is gone, and I tilt back in the chair, balancing on the back legs; my body is still, and numb,

and glancing upward, I notice the crossbeam, a tremendous piece of oak, hand-hewn, that divides the attic over my desk . . . something associated with it comes to mind, and in a moment I recall

the tornado

We had seen it coming from the front porch, and my father had herded us—Mother, Carl and myself—into the basement, while he went first to the barn to secure a logging chain, and then returned to the house, and climbed (we could hear his footsteps, the chain clanking on the stairs behind him) to the attic . . . then there was silence, save for the rising wind. I was little then, easily held by the wrist, but Carl, whining and squirming, suddenly broke away, and before he could be reached he had jumped the steps three at a time and was gone . . . Mother screamed after him, but didn't follow: she tightened her grip on me, and let him go. The house fairly shook, we heard the barn roof lifting and settling in the pasture, some of the other outbuildings collapsing, and we thought for a moment that the roof of the house had been moved . . . After it was over, Father would say little, except to command Carl to what was left of the barn for punishment . . .

but Carl—the excitement of the storm mixed with the tears of his beating—couldn't wait to tell me what had happened: how Father had lifted planks, had secured one end of the chain to floor beams, the other to the cross-beam overhead; how the roof had started to lift, and the chain had held—but the second time, the chain had broken, and Father had grasped an end in each hand . . .

. . . when the roof lifted a third time, Father had spreadeagled himself, his feet off the floor, the whole superstructure held by his hands, arms and shoulders . . .

> (*Melville: "And prove that oak, and iron, and man/Are tough in fibre yet . . ."*

The roof twisted slightly, and settled back in its old position . . .

. . . and after, Father had deliberately unfastened the chain, surveyed the broken link, restored the floor planks, and (although he had taken no notice of him, Carl had thought himself undiscovered) called to Carl, dragged him from his hiding place near the eaves, and marched him to the barn for a thrashing . . .

It was the Polar Front—meeting of Polar Continental and Tropical Maritime—that caused Columbus' dirty weather. The violent air masses, forming a circular motion . . .

> (*Bondi, Cosmology: "The nebulae show great similarity amongst themselves. They are probably all rotating and many of them show*

68

. . . create a hurricane, or perhaps tornado or waterspout, a sucking up . . .

But Columbus, first and always a navigator, fought it out . . .

and Melville, too, whose eye was level . . .

> *(". . . let me look into a human eye; it is*
> *better than to gaze upon God."*

. . . went—not up—but sounding, into the whirlpool, the vortex . . .

. . . went down.

> ". . . *resuming his horizontal attitude, Moby-Dick swam swiftly*
> *round and round the wrecked crew; sideways churning the water*
> *in his vengeful wake, as if lashing himself up to still another and*
> *more deadly assault. The sight of the splintered boat seemed to*
> *madden him . . . Meanwhile Ahab half smothered in the foam of*
> *the whale's insolent tail, and too much of a cripple to swim,—*
> *though he could still keep afloat, even in the heart of such a*
> *whirlpool as that; helpless Ahab's head was seen, like a tossed*
> *bubble . . ."*

> *The vortex: ". . . whose centre had now become the old man's*
> *head."*

T W O

Hur obed, the Phoenician sailors called it: hole of perdition . . .

Charybdis.

And on the second voyage, Columbus, sailing along the southern coast of Cuba, suddenly "entered a white sea, which was as white as milk, and as thick as the water in which tanners treat their skins." The colors changed—white, green, crystal-clear, to black—and the men recalled old Arabic tales of the Green Sea of Gloom, and endless shoals that fringed the edge of the world.

"... there was no room to shoot up into the wind and anchor; nor was there holding ground ..."

Carib Charybdis—such, perhaps, as Hart Crane—the ocean already in his head—leaped into ...

First voyage, return: "All night they were beating to windward, and going as near as they could, so as to see some way to the island at sunrise. That night the Admiral got a little rest, for he had not slept nor been able to sleep since Wednesday, and he had lost the use of his legs from long exposure to the wet and cold."

And elsewhere, contending with cannibals:
"The barbarians, being only three men with two women and a single Indian captive ... persevered in seeking safety by swimming, in which art they are skilful. At last they were captured and taken to the Admiral. One of them was pierced through in seven places and his intestines protruded from his wounds. Since it was believed that he could not be healed, he was thrown into the sea. But emerging to the surface, with one foot upraised, and with his left hand holding his intestines in their place, he swam courageously towards the shore. This caused great alarm to the Indians who were brought along as interpreters ... The Cannibal was therefore recaptured near the shore, bound hand and foot more tightly, and again thrown headlong into the sea. This resolute barbarian swam still more eagerly towards the shore, till, transpierced with many arrows, he at length expired."

Reaching Portugal, "... they were told that such a winter, with as many storms, had never before been known, and that 25 ships had been lost in Flanders ..."

And on Española, at Navidad, a few Spaniards had been left behind, the first colonists: "These, fighting bravely to the last, when they could no longer withstand the attack of the thronged battalions of their foes, were at length cut to pieces. The information conveyed ... was confirmed by the discovery of the dead bodies of ten Spaniards. These bodies were emaciated and ghastly, covered with dust and bespattered with blood, discoloured, and retaining still a fierce aspect. They had lain now nearly three months neglected and unburied under the open air."

Moby-Dick: "*At length as the craft was cast to one side, and ran ranging along with the White Whale's flank, he seemed strangely oblivious of its advance—as the whale sometimes will—and Ahab was fairly within the smoky mountain mist, which, thrown off from the whale's spout, curled round his great Monadnock hump; he was even thus close to him; when, with body arched back, and both arms lengthwise high-lifted to the poise ...*"

(Melville, elsewhere: "... since all human affairs are subject to organic disorder, since they are created in and sustained by a sort of half-disciplined chaos, hence he who in great things seeks success must never wait for smooth water, which never was and never will be, but, with what straggling method he can, dash with all his derangements at his object ..."

"... he darted his fierce iron, and his far fiercer curse into the whale."

The medical book: "Once within the periphery of the ovum, the sperm's head and neck detach from its tail which may be left wholly outside and in no case plays any part in the events to follow. The head next rotates 180° and proceeds toward the centre of the egg where the egg nucleus, having finished the maturative divisions, awaits it. During this journey the sperm head enlarges, becomes open-structured, and is converted into the male pronucleus."

The head enlarges, becomes open-structured ... I tilt forward, the front legs of the chair striking the floor, and then turn to face the far end, the western end of the attic ... turning, then, completely around, I face the desk again, and become dizzy ...

Moby-Dick: "And now, concentric circles seized the lone boat itself, and all its crew, and each floating oar, and every lance-pole, and spinning, animate and inanimate, all round and round in one vortex, carried the smallest chip of the Pequod out of sight."

(Melville, elsewhere: "... in tremendous extremities human souls are like drowning men; well enough they know they are in peril; well enough they know the causes of that peril;—nevertheless, the sea is the sea, and these drowning men do drown."

To Hawthorne: "The Whale is completed."

But the waters came pouring in, rushing and filling:

> *"My dear Hawthorne, the atmospheric skepticisms steal into me now, and make me doubtful of my sanity . . ."*

and

> *". . . let us add Moby Dick to our blessing, and step from that. Leviathan is not the biggest fish;—I have heard of Krakens."*

> (a sea-monster, mile and a half in circumference, darkening the ocean with a black liquid, and causing a gigantic whirlpool when it sinks . . .

> *Moby-Dick:* *"Now small fowls flew screaming over the yet yawning gulf; a sullen white surf beat against its steep sides; then all collapsed, and the great shroud of the sea rolled on as it rolled five thousand years ago."*

. . . rolled on over Herman Melville, his compatriots and descendants, who breathed and wrote, thenceforth, from within the ocean.

But there was that which followed after the closing of the waters: there was the family . . .

Lizzie, wife to Herman, and counterpole to Fayaway . . .

> (with Columbus—discoverer, beginner— the order was reversed: wife first, and then mistress . . .

. . . struggling to help by copying Mardi (whose fogs she could not penetrate), and

> *"My cold is very bad indeed, perhaps worse than it has ever been so early . . ."*

There was the bond:

Lizzie, whose mother died in delivering her, and who might have said to herself, "I killed my mother"; and who, having been thus abandoned, would have been strongly averse to abandoning Herman . . .

Lizzie, who, like Hart Crane, suffered from hay fever, and thus, wet-headed, mourned her mother . . .

and Herman, as Jonah, swallowed by a white monster—Herman, who might have said: "My mother killed me" . . .

> (*and Maria Melville, as Mrs. Glendinning:*
> "*I feel now as though I had borne the last of*
> *a swiftly to be extinguished race . . .*"

In any case—love, prestige, privation—they were established: Lizzie and Herman . . . Mr. & Mrs. Herman Melville . . . Mr. H. Melville, & wife.

And there were the children:
Mackey,
Stanny,
Bessie,
& Fanny,

hovering at the edge of the storm, the vortex, and

killed, crippled or withered, according to the order of birth, to how near in time (the father's space) they came

to the eye of it.

Melville—as good a parent as, say, Columbus was an administrator—was more of a prophet:

> *There was the letter to Mackey, 1860:* "*Whilst the sailors were aloft on one of the yards, the ship rolled and plunged terribly; and it blew with sleet and hail, and was very cold & biting. Well, all at once, Uncle Tom saw something falling through the air, and then heard a thump, and then,—looking before him, saw a poor sailor lying dead on the deck. He had fallen from the yard, and was killed instantly.*"

> **(Mackey, you shall die violently** . . .

> *And the letter written by Stanny, as a little boy, to his grand-mother:* "*Papa took me to the cattle show grounds to see the soldiers drill, but we did not see them, . . . it was too bad. But papa took me a ride all through the Cemetary.*"

> **(Stanny, you shall die quietly** . . .

*And the letter Melville wrote to Bessie, 1860: "Many [sea-birds]
have followed the ship day after day . . . they were all over speckled
—and they would sometimes, during a calm, keep behind the
ship, fluttering about in the water, with a mighty cackling, and
wherever anything was thrown overboard they would hurry to
get it. But they would never light on the ship—they kept all the
time flying or else resting themselves by floating on the water like
ducks in a pond. These birds have no home, unless it is some
wild rocks in the middle of the ocean."*

<u>(Bessie, you shall be homeless . . .</u>

And the children responded:

Mackey, age 18, young dog, fond of firearms, who slept with a pistol
under his pillow—came home one night at 3 a.m., and failed to rise in
the morning.

*"Time went on and Herman advised Lizzie to let him sleep, be
late at the office & take the consequences as a sort of punishment . . ."*

*". . . in the evening, the door of the room was opened, and young
Melville was found dead, lying on the bed, with a single-barrelled
pistol firmly grasped in his right hand, and a pistol-shot wound in
the right temple."*

> *(Melville: "I wish you could have seen him
> as he lay in his last attitude, the ease of a
> gentle nature.")*

*And the funeral: ". . . the young Volunteer Company to which
Malcolm belonged & who had asked the privilege of being present
& carrying the coffin from the house to the cars—filed in at one
door from the hall & out at the other—each pausing for an instant to look at the face of their lost comrade. Cousin Helen says
they were all <u>so young</u> & it was really a sadly beautiful sight—
for the cold limbs of the dead wore the same garments as the strong
active ones of the living—Cousin Lizzie—his almost heart broken
Mother having dressed her eldest son in the new suit he had taken
such pride & pleasure in wearing—Four superb wreaths and
crosses of the choicest white flowers were placed on the coffin . . ."*

And after, the family pondered whether it was suicide or accident, not thinking that Mackey had held the pistol, and Mackey had pulled the trigger—

the only question being whether he had been conscious of his actions, of his motives.

And there was Stanny:

> *"My deafness has been a great trouble to me lately . . ."*

> > (What was he trying to drown out—the brother's gunshot? . . . the family arguments? . . . or:

> *Stanwix: "I fear it will give you but little pleasure to hear from one, who has been guilty of so many follies, and deaf to the counsel of older heads."*

> *And: "Stanwix is full of the desire to go to sea, & see something of this great world. He used to talk to me about it, but I always tried to talk him out of it. But now he seems so bent upon it, that Herman & Lizzie have given their consent, thinking that one voyage to China will cure him of the fancy."*

But it took more than one voyage to cure his father . . .

> *"What have you heard of Stanwix Melville from what point did he run away? & where was his place of destination? Poor Cousin Lizzie She will be almost broken hearted."*

A shadow of his father, even to the running away . . . or perhaps, simply, escaping the disaster . . .

> *Later: "You know I left New York in April & went to a small town in Kansas, I staid there a few weeks, then I thought I could do better South so I came down through the Indian Nation, & then into Arkansas, I stopped at a number of towns on the Arkansas river till I came to the Mississippi, then down that river to Vicksburgh I staid there a few days, & then took the train to Jackson, from there by Railroad to New Orleans, I found that a lively city, but no work, so I thought I should like a trip to Central America, I went on a steamer to Havana, Cuba & from there to half a dozen or more ports on the Central America coast till I came to Limon Bay in Costa Rica."*

Columbus, fourth voyage, off Central America: "It was one continual rain, thunder and lightning. The ships lay exposed to the weather, with sails torn, and anchors, rigging, cables, boats and many of the stores lost; the people exhausted . . . Other tempests I have seen, but none that lasted so long or so grim as this. Many old hands whom we looked on as stout fellows lost their courage. . . . I was sick and many times lay at death's door, but gave orders from a dog-house that the people clapped together for me on the poop deck."

Rounding Cabo Gracia á Dios, he was able to coast southward to what is now called Limon Bay, in Costa Rica, where he anchored and rested for ten days.

Stanny: "I walked from there on the beach with two other young fellows to Greytown in Nicaragua, one of the boys died on the beach, & we dug a grave in the sand by the sea, & buried him, & travelled on again, each of us not knowing who would have to bury the other before we got there, as we were both sick with the fever & ague."

Columbus drifted down the coast, searching for a passage, a channel to the Red Sea . . .

(Plato, describing Atlantis: ". . . and drove a canal through the zones of land three hundred feet in width, about a hundred feet deep, and about sixty miles in length. At the landward end of this waterway, which was capable of navigation by the largest vessels, they constructed a harbour. The two zones of land were cut by large canals, by which means a trireme, or three-decked galley, was able to pass from one sea-zone to another."

Stanny: "I went up the San Juan river to Lake Nicaragua about a hundred miles with a Naval surveying expedition going up to survey for a ship Canal . . ."

. . . searching for a canal, a short-cut, to avoid the rigours of the long voyage . . .

(*Melville, commenting on Emerson: "To one who has weathered Cape Horn as a common sailor what stuff all this is."*

Stanny: ". . . from Greytown I shipped on a schooner for Aspinwall; after arriving in Aspinwall, I got wrecked there in that heavy gale of wind . . . and I lost all my clothes, & every thing I had, & was taken sick again with the fever, I went into the hospital there, & then came home on the Steamer Henry Chauncey, where I find the cold weather agrees with me much better, than the sun of the tropics.

Now I say New York forever."

Later: "I am happy to announce to you that this morning I went to work for a dentist, a Dr. Read; I went to his office on Saturday, & told him I wanted a place to work & perfect myself in the profession . . ."

<u>Moby-Dick</u>: *"With a long, weary hoist the jaw is dragged on board, as if it were an anchor; and when the proper time comes— some few days after the other work—Queequeg, Dagoo, and Tashtego, being all accomplished dentists, are set to drawing teeth. With a keen cutting-spade, Queequeg lances the gums; then the jaw is lashed down to ringbolts, and a tackle being rigged from aloft, they drag out these teeth, as Michigan oxen drag stumps of old oaks out of wild wood-lands."*

And in <u>Mardi</u>, the cannibals wore teeth as ornaments, and hoarded them as money—teeth, like money, being the means of eating . . .

> *(Stanny: ". . . in a few years I will be independent of any man."*

But: "I have encountered a serious obstacle which will prevent me from becoming a number one dentist, & that is I am too near sighted; I found it out as quick as I commenced operating in the mouth . . . I am going to sail Wednesday for San Francisco . . ."

Lizzie: "We have better news from Stanny—He is on a sheep-ranch in California . . ."

And: "I wanted to tell you that we are expecting Stanny home in a short time—A very favorable opening for his going back to his old business, <u>mechanical</u> dentistry offered itself . . ."

"Stanny begs me to thank you very much for all your kind wishes—he is very well now (with the exception of a little bowel trouble) . . ."

1875, departs for San Francisco, and

"There is a party of five or six of us that are going to start for the

*Black Hills country about the middle or last of January . . . I
have made up my mind, this is a chance, & I may be lucky there,
at any rate I can get miners wages which is more than I can make
here . . . and I am going this winter if I die of starvation or get
frozen to death on the road.”*

*Lizzie: “I have been writing to Stanny . . . he has been sick poor
fellow, and had to go in the hospital at Sacramento . . .”*

*“We hear constantly from Stanny—I wish I could say he is
materially better . . .”*

*“. . . a good deal worried about Stanny’s health—his pulmonary
troubles have been worse . . .”*

and Melville, now age 66—whose own paternity had been blasted,
who had been thrust loose in an earlier world—signs a letter to Stanny:

> **Good bye, & God bless you**
> **Your affectionate Father**
> **H. Melville.**

A death notice:

MELVILLE—At San Francisco, Cal., 23ᵈ inst., Stanwix, son of Herman and
Elizabeth S. Melville, in the 35th year of his age.

And there was Bessie, third-born, and oldest daughter:

thin, small, weak-voiced, but with a sharp tongue (she liked raw
humor),

crippled with arthritis (they never saw such feet on one who could
still walk), afraid of strong winds, afraid that she would be blown
over . . .

lived with her mother, and then alone, an old maid (she didn’t like
little children, couldn’t stand their little smelly drawers),

and when she died, quarts of black liquid—undigested food—were
found in her system . . .

And finally, Fanny, last-born, furthest removed from the disaster,

who salvaged life and fertility (she married a man from Philadelphia,
and gave birth to four daughters . . .

who nevertheless had her own troubles (and blamed them all on her father . . .

developed arthritis (she could be seen on the porch of her summer home, Edgartown—white-headed, her sweet, gentle face, white, she in a white dress—her leg out stiff, arthritic . . .

and died, finally, incontinent and placid, a baby—1935.

Thus the four children of Herman Melville:

The men:

one, dead by his own hand, and the other, wasted . . .

> (*Melville, as Pierre: "Lo! I leave corpses wherever I go!"*

And the women:

arthritic, motionless, holding against the down-rushing waters . . .

And hovering over all, moving, surviving, through the long term of Melville's life, and beyond—was Lizzie . . .

Shifting again, I glance, not upward, as at the crossbeam, but downward, between my legs, at the floor . . . and I recall (my arms and legs are tense, a little tired, as though strained) waiting in the basement, alone with Mother, during the tornado . . . the loneliness, the wanting to be with Carl, wanting to be, as he was, up in the rigging, in the storm, with Father—and having to wait, instead, in the darkness, in the grip that I was too young to break . . . lifting my eyes level again, I read

that the bride of Columbus in all probability did not survive five years of the marriage; and

> "Not the slightest hint has come down to us of the appearance or disposition of Columbus's only wife; Dona Felipa is as shadowy a figure as the Discoverer's mother."

> (About Melville's wife, and mother, a great deal is known . . .

Whether dead or still living, Dona Felipa was abandoned when Columbus left Portugal.

And on the first voyage, early in the return, Columbus set out to discover the island of <u>Matinino</u>, inhabited, as the Indians told him, only by women; for this might be Marco Polo's <u>Feminea</u> . . .

. . . but the ships were leaking, and the wind blew strong from the west: he changed his course for Spain.

> Third voyage: ". . . at the lengthe an Eastsoutheaste wynde arose, and gave a prosperous blaste to his sayles." . . . the fleet coasted before the trades, through "El Golfo de las Damas," the Ladies' Sea . . .

> *And Melville, late in life, in a letter: "But you do not know, perhaps, that I have already entered my eighth decade. After twenty years nearly, as an outdoor Customs House officer, I have latterly come into possession of unobstructed leisure, but only just as, in the course of nature, my vigor sensibly declines."*

Columbus, on the third voyage, executed one of the most extraordinary feats of dead-reckoning navigation: Margarita (The Terrestrial Paradise) to Hispaniola . . .

and arriving, troubled with gout, found the colony disorganized, Roldan in rebellion . . . and instead of clean action, fighting and subduing Roldan, he negotiated, submitted to a set of humiliating agreements . . .

> *(Fanny, describing Melville, his later peacefulness: "He just didn't have the energy any more . . ."*

. . . and later he was put in fetters (darbies, Melville called them) and sent back to Spain, on what proved to be the only eastward voyage, return voyage, accompanied by any sort of good weather . . .

> (on shipboard, they offered to take off the fetters, but he refused, declared that he would wear them until he had the opportunity to kneel with them still on, before the Sovereigns. Ever after this, he guarded them jealously, kept them in his room, directed that they be interred with his body . . .

> *Melville, reading Homer, checks and underscores: "The work that I was born to do is done!"*

After the Civil War, when Franco had won, Carl teamed with a Span-

ish family, four brothers and a sister: Rico, Rafael, Salomón, Diego and Concha—old Spanish aristocrats (though they had been fighting, so Carl claimed, for the Loyalists). All wanted to get out of Spain (the Spaniards complained that no one spoke Spanish, it was all Russian and German), so they acquired a yacht and set sail for Cuba . . .

. . . where Carl lived for several years, becoming embroiled in one after another of the rebellions. One by one, three of the four brothers (Rico alone escaped) were destroyed, aligning themselves on different sides in the fighting . . . Carl carried with him a photo of Rafael, his shirt torn, his body spattered with blood, lying drenched in sunlight on the pavement, where he had fallen . . . it came out (when Carl was drunk) that they had been fighting on opposite sides, and that perhaps it had been Carl's own gun that had killed him . . .

We heard little of Concha, she was studying medicine, and was quiet, but she fought side by side with the men . . . and Carl seemed to be always where she was . . .

THE INDES

ONE

COLUMBUS, in the original capitulations—a set of outrageous demands imposed upon the Sovereigns, before undertaking the first voyage—refers to "the things requested and which Your Highnesses give and grant Don Cristóbal Colón, as some satisfaction for what he has discovered in the ocean seas, and of the voyage which now, with the help of God, he is to undertake through those seas in the service of Your Highnesses."

... the man from Genoa, at a time when the Indes existed only as spots in his own wild imaginings, referring to them as "what he has discovered" ...

> (as the Azores were first pulled out
> of the ocean by Portuguese, in search of
> St. Brandon's ...

There is a law of excess, of abundance, whereby a people must explore the ocean, in order to be competent on land ...

> (*Melville: "You must have plenty of*
> *sea-room to tell the Truth in ..."*

Men must put out space, and nations ships ...

> *Columbus, reported by a contemporary: "... the said Admiral*
> *always went beyond the bounds of truth in reporting his own*
> *affairs."*

> *and Typee, Melville's first book, was first rejected because "it was*
> *impossible that it could be true and therefore was without real*
> *value" ...*

Columbus: "I hold it for certain that the waters of the sea move from east to west with the sky, and that in passing this track they hold a more rapid course, and have thus carried away large tracts of land, and that from hence has resulted this great number of islands; indeed these islands themselves afford an additional proof of it, for all of them, without exception, run lengthwise, from west to east . . ."

Sitting forward in my chair, I am aware of energy flows in my body—nerve sensations, something that feels like accelerated blood circulation—as though internal balances, relationships, centres of control have been disturbed. Pushing the chair back, I stand up, leaning forward slightly, my arms limp, and give the sensation full play . . . in the matter of balance, I am aware almost at once of the clubfoot: there is the old anger, the hatred, the desire to amputate the monstrous member . . .

Slumping in the chair, I let the anger rankle in me . . . my blood is warm, and begins to move more thickly . . .

As the anger diminishes, there is left the warmth, and again, the disturbance, the imbalance, and something erotic . . .

Columbus: "In Cariay and the neighboring country there are great enchanters of a very fearful character. They would have given the world to prevent my remaining there an hour. When I arrived they sent me immediately two girls very showily dressed; the eldest could not be more than eleven years of age, and the other seven, and both exhibited so much immodesty that more could not be expected from public women; they carried concealed about them a magic powder . . ."

Elsewhere: "They afterwards came to the ship's boats where we were, swimming and bringing us parrots, cotton threads in skeins, darts, and many other things . . ."

"Here the fish are so unlike ours that it is wonderful. Some are the shape of dories, and of the finest colors in the world, blue, yellow, red, and other tints, all painted in various ways, and the colors are so bright that there is not a man who would not be astonished, and would take great delight in seeing them."

". . . the women have very pretty bodies, and they were the first to

*bring what they had, especially things to eat, bread made of yams,
and shrivelled quinces . . ."*

Rising, pushing back the chair, I step to my left, leading with the club
. . . but the stride is strange. There is something other than the old sensation of heel and ball, in the false boot, striking the floor: an over- or
under-balance in a different direction . . . as though the right foot were
clubbed, globular and more monstrous than the left. I pause, and re-
treat, my hands reaching back for the arms of the chair . . . and am
scarcely seated again before the third leg, the middle leg—clubbed in
its own way—hardens and rises . . .

but this is not all: I am refreshed, my body renewed: remaining still,
leaning back in the chair, I become aware of different locations, different sources from which motion might originate, from which my
body might begin to move: shoulder, thigh, elbow, knee—random
centres never before used, or neglected and atrophied . . . and as I
consider each, fresh energy comes into me, and the old centred leg
subsides . . .

Columbus:

> *"This said island of Juana is exceedingly fertile, as, indeed, are
> all the others; it is surrounded with many bays, spacious, very
> secure and surpassing any that I have ever seen; numerous large
> and healthful rivers intersect it, and it also contains many very
> lofty mountains. All these islands are very beautiful, and dis-
> tinguished by a diversity of scenery; they are filled with a great
> variety of trees of immense height, and which I believe to retain
> their foliage in all seasons; for when I saw them they were as
> verdant and luxuriant as they usually are in Spain in the month
> of May—some of them were blossoming, some bearing fruit, and
> all flourishing in the greatest perfection, according to their re-
> spective stages of growth, and the nature and quality of each: yet
> the islands are not so thickly wooded as to be impassable. The
> nightingale and various birds were singing in countless numbers,
> and that in November, the month in which I arrived there. There
> are, besides, in the same island of Juana, seven or eight kinds of
> palm trees, which, like all the other trees, herbs and fruits, con-
> siderably surpass ours in height and beauty. The pines, also, are
> very handsome, and there are very extensive fields and meadows,
> a variety of birds, different kinds of honey . . ."*

"... there are mountains of very great size and beauty, vast plains, groves, and very fruitful fields, admirably adapted for tillage, pasture and habitation. The convenience and excellence of the harbors in this island, so indispensable to the health of man, surpass anything that would be believed by one who had not seen it."

"The island of Española is preeminent in beauty and excellence, offering to the sight the most enchanting view of mountains, plains, rich fields for cultivation, and pastures for flocks of all sorts, with situations for towns and settlements. Its harbours are of such excellence that their description would not gain belief, and the like may be said of its abundance of large and fine rivers ..."

"In all this district there are very high mountains which seem to reach the sky ... and they are all green with trees. Between them there are very delicious valleys."

"He said that all he saw was so beautiful that his eyes could never tire of gazing on such loveliness, nor his ears of listening to the songs of birds."

and there was the review of Melville's Mardi: "Wild similes, cloudy philosophy, all things turned topsy-turvy, until we seem to feel all earth melting away from beneath our feet, and nothing but Mardi remaining ..."

Dr. Chanca, reporting on the second voyage: "Thus, surely, their Highnesses the King and Queen may henceforth regard themselves as the most prosperous and wealthy sovereigns in the world; never yet, since the creation, has such a thing been seen or read of ..."

T W O

Glancing at the books, reaching for my handkerchief to re-arrange the dust among them, I become, for a moment, the pale Usher, at the very beginning of Moby-Dick: "... Threadbare in coat, heart, body, and brain; I see him now. He was ever dusting his old lexicons and grammars, with a queer handkerchief, mockingly embellished with all the gay flags of all the known nations of the world. He loved to dust his old grammars; it somehow mildly reminded him of his mortality."

Musing for a moment, the dusty handkerchief in hand, my body relaxed, refreshed, waiting for something, I read that on a certain cruise away from Isabella, Columbus was constantly on duty, day and night, at one time going thirty-two days without sleep. He suddenly became ill, suffering a pestilential fever and a drowsiness or supreme stupor which totally deprived him of all his forces and senses, so that he was believed to be dying.

> *Melville, in a letter: "For my part, I love sleepy fellows, and the more ignorant the better. Damn your wideawake and knowing chaps. As for sleepiness, it is one of the noblest qualities of humanity. There is something sociable about it, too. Think of those sensible and sociable millions of good fellows all taking a good long snooze together, under the sod . . ."*

Musing, still, I think of islands, of the meaning of islands . . .

. . . of the Aegean, the Indes, and Polynesia . . .

and the endings in islands: Antillia disintegrating, perhaps, into the Indes, and Atlantis, into the Canaries, Azores and Cape Verdes . . .

There was Melville, an old man, 104 East Twenty-Sixth Street: withdrawn into family, books and private publications: lonely as Hunilla on the Encantadas, the enchanted islands: insular on Manhattan . . .

and Columbus, back in Spain, in Valladolid, shunted from the Court, alone, crippled with gout . . .

(from the medical book:

called in the old days the "Disease of Diana," because it afflicted hunters, gout is arthritic in type, resulting from imperfect excretion of uric acid. It occurs more often in spring and autumn—the seasons of change.

> "The disturbance of uric acid metabolism causes an over-saturation of urates in the blood . . . Crystalline deposits formed will . . . act as centers for further precipitation of the over-saturated fluids.
> In the bone-marrow below the endochondral junction, small deposits of urate crystals may be found . . ."

. . . the Indes, lost to Columbus now that they had become actual, were repossessed, precipitated once more from his imagination into the extremities of his body—the joints of his toes—as he had precipi-

tated them before into the extremities of the known world: the islands
once more his, as crystals . . .

THREE

Beyond the attic is the wind, and beyond that, the sounds of the city,
a general hum, a background, through which breaks the midnight
whistle at General Motors, announcing the graveyard . . .

> *"Twelve o'clock! It is the natural centre, key-stone, and very heart
> of the day. At that hour, the sun has arrived at the top of his hill;
> and as he seems to hang poised there a while, before coming down
> on the other side, it is but reasonable to suppose that he is then
> stopping to dine . . ."*

Melville, describing the other twelve, the sunny one . . .

Linda will soon be home—she gets a ride in an old Plymouth, the back
door hanging loose from the hinges, with some people who live beyond
us, in what may still be described as country . . .

The wind turns the north corner, and whistles under the eaves . . .
leaning back in the chair, stretching my limbs, I experience wellbeing,
as though I had just dined . . . I reach for an inner pocket, and take out
a fine cigar, given me yesterday by the superintendent at the plant. I
prolong the ritual: removing the cellophane, sniffing the weed, and
lighting up . . .

> *Las Casas: ". . . and having lighted one part of it, by the other they
> suck, absorb or receive that smoke inside with the breath, by which
> they become benumbed and almost drunk, and so it is said that
> they do not feel fatigue. These muskats, as we call them, they call
> tobacco."*

Withdrawing the cigar, holding it before me, I inspect it, the crafts-
manship of it, and think of the Indian canoes, made of "very tall,
large, long and odoriferous red cedars . . ."

Leaning forward again, the cigar now fixed in the corner of my mouth,
I read

of dexter and sinister: the old words for right and left . . .

to the Greeks, whose gods resided in the north, the word for right also
meant east, the word for left west . . .

and in Mayan mummification, white was associated with the north
and the lungs, yellow with the south and the belly, red with the east
and larger intestines, black with the west and the lesser intestines . . .

There was Columbus, making the "Pilot's blessing": arm raised, with
flattened palm between the eyes, pointing at Polaris, the North Star
. . . the arm then brought straight down to the compass card, to see if
the needle varied . . .

. . . or telling time, by checking the rotation of the Guards, two bright-
est stars of the Dipper, around Polaris . . . the time being determined
by where the principal Guard appeared on the chart: West Shoulder,
East Arm, Line below West Arm, or East Shoulder . . .

As I sit here, facing east, crouching over the desk, north and south at
my elbows, my back to the west, I read

(Columbus)

> ". . . *that the world of which I speak is different from that in
> which the Romans, and Alexander, and the Greeks made mighty
> efforts with great armies to gain possession of.*"

Columbus, extending himself, stretching against the contractile tensions of the known world, became a world to himself,

exasperating his fellow-pilots, in any navigational dispute, because he
invariably turned out right, even his errors, gross as they were, being
more accurate than those of the others; and his unreasonable and least
accurate presumptions had a way of meeting compensations, that
made the results of these presumptions correct . . .

. . . proud and arrogant, demanding (second voyage) more honors than
those by which he was already overwhelmed . . . suspicious and dis-
trustful, breaking, one by one, with all his associates: Pinzon, Fonseca,
Buil, Margarite, Aguado . . .

> (as Melville broke with Hawthorne,
> Duyckink . . .

. . . unable to understand the Spaniards, who clamored to join him on the second voyage out, and who must therefore (he thought) desire to establish a permanent colony in the Indes . . .

> (but who only wanted to get their rape, gold, slaves and the hell home to Spain, so that on the second voyage, return, the Niña and the India, each designed for a complement of 25 men, carried a total of 255 . . .

Stranded,

like Melville (whose family all made attempts to "bring him out of himself":

> *"I am as deeply impressed as you possibly can be of the necessity of Herman's getting away from Pitts. He is there solitary, without society, without exercise or occupation except that which is very likely to be injurious to him in over-straining his mind."*

> *Lizzie: "The fact is, that Herman, poor fellow, is in such a frightfully nervous state . . . that I am actually afraid to have any one here for fear that he will be upset entirely . . ."*

There is a commotion on the stairs, voices: one of them seems to be Linda, and I get the sense that she is going in two directions—her footsteps ascending (the old stairs creaking under her weight), while her voice goes down the stairwell, to one of the children.

I am confused, the midnight whistle has only just blown, Linda couldn't possibly be home . . . off-balance, I stumble as I get up, nearly tipping the chair,

pause to set the cigar carefully on the table-edge, and then go to the door . . .

    "Michael . . ."

There is at once, as I open the door, before the word is spoken, the view, the perception (the door swinging darkly, from right to left)—what I see:

Linda, standing midway on the stairs, perhaps a little nearer the top, her feet close together, her body, her attention turned (as I had felt) in two directions: not twisted or unnatural, but, in the disposition of her feet, her hips, her shoulders, her head, a tendency of motion: partly upward, toward me, and partly down the stairs, toward Mike Jr., the oldest child,

who stands near the bottom, his motion or rather his stillness likewise tentative: ready to climb or withdraw, so that he seems peeking from behind himself. His right foot is advanced to the tread above, his head tilted slightly; and I guess at the look in his face, hidden within the oversized plastic space helmet (he insisted on getting the large one), which makes his head seem a great gray globe, nearly as large as his trunk, with vast space between the plastic and the boy. In his hand he holds (I remember the cereal-box-tops collected and squirreled away on kitchen shelves until the necessary accompanying dimes and quarters could be accumulated) the cosmic atomic space gun, green, with concentric circles on the handle and the barrel—the gun pointed upward, not directly, but vaguely, toward his father.

> "Michael, what have you been doing? What's the meaning of this?"

> "What . . .?" (still holding the door, my body erect, so that an iron-like firmness runs up from the clubfoot through the knee-joint, the hip, the shoulder, and down through the arm, to the brass knob) ". . . the meaning of what?"

> "Michael . . ."

. . . and as she begins to speak, to act, moving her body, swinging her arm in a small arc (as large as the stairwell permits) I endeavor to sort out the feelings, the emotions that slam into me. There is her appearance: short, like myself, a little shorter than I, and getting stout, so that her stomach protrudes, just below the belt of her dress—protrudes further than her breasts; her feet small, her feet and legs that seem to go so well with any floor, pavement or ground on which she stands, so that however tired she may become, however sagging her posture, she seems to belong to and celebrate, be it in grace or in weariness, the act of standing; her arms, seeming to grow shorter as they gain more flesh; and her head, her face, not pretty now because she is complaining, but, in all its plainness (the blond-auburn curls hanging in disarray over the steel-rimmed glasses, and her eyes, blue, set wide apart, not angry, but simply committed to an act, a gesture, committed to and facing and participating in it) a great delicacy that, even now, as so often in the past, I find compelling . . .

> "Michael, every light in the house is bɪ ˙ng, the children are in an uproar, the television going . .

> Mike Jr. (gains confidence, takes a step up—the voice muffled): "Jenifer's crying!"

> Linda: "What have you been doing?"

and, not waiting for an answer,

> "I came home early, I had to tell the foreman I was ill, because I knew something was wrong, I just felt that thinɡ weren't right . . ."

and

"I suppose we'll have to hire a sitter . . ."

Relaxing my hold on the doorknob, I shift balance to the other foot, take a step, a gesture toward her,

"Linda . . . I'm sorry . . . I didn't know . . ."

and before I say more she turns away from me, careful to reject what I have to say before I say it, and for this I feel no annoyance, neither at her failure nor mine, but only a great stupid sort of pity for both of us . . .

> **Linda (turns downstairs, her voice snapping): "Mike Jr! Get down there! Into your bed!"**

. . . angry now, because she doesn't want to, will not, cannot face what is with me . . .. The boy vanishes with the crack of her syllables, and

> **Linda (turning at the bottom of the stairs, her words pointed, not directly, but vaguely, toward me): "After all, the kids have to get up for school tomorrow, and you have to work . . ."**

Without speaking, I start down the stairs, but again, quickly, she stops me:

> **"Never mind . . ." (her back turned toward me, her feet now on the floor below**
>
> **and I: "Linda . . ."**
>
> **then she, turning partly toward me again): "I'm home now . . . (and closes the door at the bottom of the stairs).**

Pausing, pivoting on the club, my hand on the rail, I stand in the near dark—the only light being that which spills, many times reflected and diminished, through the open doorway above.

For some moments, I am still.

Turning, then, completing the half-circle pivot, I glance at the stair-treads above, and take a step upward, the right foot leading, the left dragging heavily behind . . .

> *(Melville: "But live & push—tho' we put one leg forward ten miles—it's no reason the other must lag behind—no, that must again distance the other—& so we go till we get the cramp . . ."*

Reaching the upper floor again, the old planks, I pause and look around, to re-create the dimensions of the attic. Walking to the desk,

I am conscious of the act, the motions and sounds I make, as on a voyage: the few steps across the boards, from the head of the stairs to the desk. I pick up the cigar, draw on it, and stand for some moments. I recall that

Columbus at first thought he had discovered India . . .

> ("*They found a large nut of the kind belonging to India, great rats, and enormous crabs. He saw many birds, and there was a strong smell of musk . . .*"

. . . thereby lopping off, roughly, one-half the globe: a hemisphere gone . . .

> *Melville, describing Hawthorne: "Still there is something lacking —a good deal lacking—to the plump sphericity of the man."*

F O U R

I have been holding my head still for some moments, and I experience something like a headache, but not quite the same . . . a wall seems to run through the middle of my head, from front to back, and all of me, the total "I", is cramped into one side, the right . . .

> *Melville, describing Ahab: "Threading its way out from among his gray hairs, and continuing right down his tawny scorched face and neck, till it disappeared in his clothing, you saw a slender rod-like mark, lividly whitish. It resembled that perpendicular seam sometimes made in the straight lofty trunk of a great tree, when the upper lightning tearingly darts down it, and without wrenching a single twig, peels and grooves out the bark from top to bottom, ere running off into the soil, leaving the tree still greenly alive, but branded. Whether that mark was born with him, or whether it was the scar left by some desperate wound, no one could certainly say."*

> *And elsewhere: "Seems to me some sort of equator cuts yon old man . . ."*

And <u>*Pierre*</u>: "... *his body contorted, and one side drooping, as though that moment halfway down-stricken with a paralysis, and yet unconscious of the stroke.*"

The vision in my left eye dims, all but disappears. I remain still, effectively blind in the left eye. Then, as suddenly as it vanished, the vision returns, starting from a central point and opening over the normal field. There remains something strange about it, however, not as before. I reach for the cigar, which I had placed on the edge of the desk, and am surprised when my hand goes beyond it. Reaching again, my hand this time falls short. There is emptiness in my stomach, and I realize what has happened: I have lost binocular vision—am unable to judge distances. It is only with the utmost care and concentration, now, that I am able to pick up the cigar.

Leaning back in the chair, smoking, I experiment with vision, let it do what it will ... but there is no change ... still the strange, two-dimensional sensation. I recall a time when Carl, late in life, experienced something similar, only apparently much worse. For a time he lost three-dimensional vision altogether, the world appearing to him as a flat plane.

> <u>*Moby-Dick*</u>: "*Now, from this peculiar sideways position of the whale's eyes, it is plain that he can never see an object which is exactly ahead, no more than he can one exactly astern. In a word, the position of the whale's eyes corresponds to that of a man's ears; and you may fancy, for yourself, how it would fare with you, did you sideways survey objects through your ears ... you would have two backs, so to speak; but, at the same time, also, two fronts (side fronts): for what is it that makes the front of a man—what, indeed, but his eyes?*"

Not only this, but Carl's eyes—set wide apart in his head—seemed to focus and move independent of one another, to receive separate images, imperfectly blended.

> "*Moreover, while in most other animals that I can now think of, the eyes are so planted as imperceptibly to blend their visual power, so as to produce one picture and not two to the brain; the peculiar position of the whale's eyes, effectually divided as they are by many cubic feet of solid head, which towers between them like a great mountain separating two lakes in valleys; this, of*

course, must wholly separate the impressions which each inde-
pendent organ imparts. The whale, therefore, must see one dis-
tinct picture on this side, and another distinct picture on that side;
while all between must be profound darkness and nothingness to
him."

He was expert in dissembling, in making his way among others without
arousing suspicion. Only a few of us who knew him well, who knew
what he was experiencing, could see him falter and waver, manipulate
others into doing things for him that he was afraid he might fumble...

"It may be but an idle whim, but it has always seemed to me, that
the extraordinary vacillations of movement displayed by some
whales when beset by three or four boats; the timidity and liability
to queer frights, so common to such whales; I think that all this
indirectly proceeds from the helpless perplexity of volition, in
which their divided and diametrically opposite powers of vision
must involve them."

The condition of my own vision remains unchanged. Smoking quietly,
musing over it, I think that in flattening the world,

as Columbus, at first, saw India for America,

> (and as others, much later, while living off
> the fat, still see only India

one loses the look of the land...

And it occurs that when the world comes in upon a man, it whirls in at
the eyes: two vortices, gouging the outlook...

Melville in Cairo: "... *multitudes of blind men—worst city in the*
world for them. Flies on the eyes at noon. Nature feeding on man."

And Columbus, fourth voyage, engaged with the natives at Belén:

Captain Diego Tristan went upstream to get fresh water, just before
the caravels were to depart—his boat was attacked by Indians, and he
was killed by a spear that went through his eye. Only one man of his
company escaped. All the corpses floated downstream, covered with
wounds, and with carrion crows circling over them, for Columbus and
his men—their ships trapped by low water inside the bar—to see.

Melville and Columbus, men of vision:

"... *my eyes, which are tender as young sparrows.*"

"... on my former voyage, when I discovered terra firma, I passed thirty-three days without natural rest, and was all that time deprived of sight ..."

"... *like an owl I steal about by twilight, owing to the twilight of my eyes.*"

"There the eyes of the Admiral became very bad from not sleeping ... he says that he found himself more fatigued here than when he discovered the island of Cuba ... because his eyes were bloodshot ..."

"... *my recovery from an acute attack of neuralgia in the eyes ...*"

"... nor did they burst and bleed as they have done now."

"... *and I felt a queer feeling in my left eye, which, as sometimes is the case with people, was the weaker one; probably from being on the same side with the heart.*"

And there was the country fellow, a relative of Mother's (she tried to deny him because he was thought to be not right in his head—lived by himself in a little shack, did odd jobs, studied strange books at night although it was thought he couldn't read, had difficulty forming thoughts in his head and passing them as words under his hare lip— but there was the name, Stonecipher, and the relationship, some sort of cousin): I remember him trying to explain to me (he used to get up early in the morning and observe the wild animals, gather herbs in the woods to sell to the neighbor women for medicines) what it is about a baby's eyesight, how it takes days or weeks after birth for the infant's eyes to focus, and gain depth perception.

"He can't ..."

> (*his great crude hand raised, the fingers spread, coming toward me, as though he were the infant, I the object to be seen, and his hand the agent of vision*

"... he can't MAKE THE OBJECT!"

> (*the fingers suddenly clutched, grasping air before my nose ... revelation and delight in his face*

96

and early one Sunday morning, when Carl and I were small boys, we went into Father's room, tried to get him to play with us. He was, or pretended to be asleep . . . we called, pulled, shoved and jounced, with no effect. We were sitting on him, out of breath, when Carl cautiously approached his face, lifted one eyelid between thumb and forefinger, and peered in. Then he turned to me, the eyelid held open as evidence:

"He's still in there."

F I V E

Genoblast,

the bisexual nucleus of the impregnated ovum.

and, the anatomy book, diagram of cell division:

> "t. End of telophase. The daughter cells are connected by the ectoplasmic stalk. The endoplasm has been completely divided by the constriction of the equatorial band. It has mixed with the interchromosomal (exnuclear) material. The compact daughter nuclei have begun to show clear areas and to enlarge. u. The daughter cells have moved in opposite directions and stretched the connecting stalk. The nuclei have larger clear areas and less visible chromosome material. v. The connecting stalk has been pulled into a thin strand by the migration of the daughter cells in opposite directions."

and

> "w. . . . The connecting stalk is broken."

Blastomere,

one of the segments into which the fertilized egg divides. And

Morula,

the mulberry mass, coral- or sponge-like, a mass of blastomeres . . . this hollows into a shell, surrounding a central cavity, and is called a

Blastosphere,

> which "becomes adherent by its embryonic pole to the epithelial lining of the uterus. There it flattens out somewhat and erodes and digests the underlying surface of the uterus."

> *(Isabel, in Pierre: "I pray for peace—for
> motionlessness—for the feeling of myself, as
> of some plant, absorbing life without seeking
> it . . ."*

and for the next two weeks the invader attacks the host, destroying epithelial
tissue to make room for itself, and set up embryotrophic nutrition.

> *Moby-Dick, The Shark Massacre: "But in the foamy confusion
> of their mixed and struggling hosts, the marksmen could not al-
> ways hit their mark; and this brought about new revelations of the
> incredible ferocity of the foe. They viciously snapped, not only at
> each other's disembowelments, but like flexible bows, bent round,
> and bit their own; till these entrails seemed swallowed over and
> over again by the same mouth, to be oppositely voided by the gap-
> ing wound."*

And on the fourth voyage of Columbus, the men, having eaten all their
supply of meat, killed some sharks. In the stomach of one, they found
the head of another, a head that they had thrown back earlier into the
sea, as being unfit to eat.

> "The trophoblast proliferates rapidly, forms a network of branching
> processes which cover the entire ovum, invade the maternal tissues and
> open into the maternal blood vessels . . ."

> (there was the Royal Order, granting am-
> nesty to all convicts who would colonize
> the Indes . . .
>
> (the new islands overrun with the undif-
> ferentiated
>
> (like the red, rushing growth that fills the
> space of a wound:
>
> (proud flesh

I shift position in the chair, my eyes having trouble with the typeface
before me . . . trying by changing the fundamental balance of my body,
of my spine, to alter what I see . . .

> "Parallel neural folds rise higher and higher, flanking the neural groove,
> and finally meet and fuse to form a closed tube which is the primordial
> brain . . ."

and there are the drawings in the medical book:

embryos, 4 to 10 weeks: the wide-set, bead-like eyes, the pig-snouts, the enormous double foreheads, grotesque, like the masks and carvings Carl acquired in Alaska . . .

> "The conclusion is that each organ not only originates from a definite embryonic area or primordium and from no other but also that it arises at a very definite moment which must be utilized then if ever."

and as I read this, the print, the black letters on white, come into sure focus. I reach to the ashtray—judging the distance with ease and pleasure—and put out the stump of my cigar.

I remain still, enjoying again a sense of refreshment, of wellbeing . . .

there is this about Columbus and Melville: both were blunt men, setting the written word on the page and letting it stand, not going back to correct their errors, not caring to be neat . . .

> (Melville: "It is impossible to talk or to write without apparently throwing one-self helplessly open . . ."

The orthography, the spelling of both was hurried, splashed with errors,

and both men annotated, scattered postils, in whatever books they read: putting islands, fragments of themselves, at the extremes of the page . . .

There was the handwriting:

Columbus, the early Columbus, man of the ocean-sea and the Indes, confident, level, forward-flowing, the touch light, the form disciplined, not flamboyant (the tops of the consonants rising and curving like Mediterranean lateen sails), exuberant,

and later, as he grew old, writing to the Sovereigns to complain and beg, the words became cramped, the letters thick, the pen bore heavily on the page, the flowing lines conflicted, became eccentric . . .

And Melville: harder, more incised (the Yankee) and crabbed, but, like Christopher, leaning forward against restraints, and on a level line: level with the horizon . . .

Whereas Columbus, complaining and failing, jabbed the page, Melville (likewise failing) withdrew from it, the pen, the thought, the man scarcely forming the word . . .

And Columbus, a very old man, all hope and islands lost to him save only as gout, as crystals at the extremities of his body, permitted his two styles to flow together and become one . . .

> (always, however, the line remaining level
> . . . the only variation being, upon occasion,
> a moderate roll, the pen riding the page
> like a caravel coasting a gentle ground
> swell, among the Indes . . .

ONE

COLUMBUS: *"In the dead of night, while I was on deck, I heard an awful roaring that came from the south, toward the ship; I stopped to observe what it might be, and I saw the sea rolling from west to east like a mountain, as high as the ship, and approaching little by little; on the top of this rolling sea came a mighty wave roaring with a frightful noise, and with all this terrific uproar were other conflicting currents, producing, as I have already said, a sound as of breakers upon the rocks. To this day I have a vivid recollection of the dread I then felt, lest the ship might founder under the force of that tremendous sea . . ."*

and Las Casas: ". . . since the force of the water is very great at all times and particularly so in this season . . . which is the season of high water, . . . and since it wants naturally to get to the sea, and the sea with its great mass under the same natural impulse wants to break upon the land, and since this gulf is enclosed by the mainland on one side and on the other side by the island . . . and since it is very narrow for such a violent force of contrary waters, it must needs be that when they meet a terrific struggle takes place and a conflict most perilous for those that find themselves in that place."

The house, the attic, are once more become a ship, but in a different sense, that of a ship struck at different points by contending waters, so that it shivers, the timbers work against one another, and the whole seems scarcely to move. I am still, and it is some moments before I realize that this sensation comes to me, not as from the timbers of the house, but as from those—the rafters, joists, sills and sleepers—of my own frame . . . my bones being of oak, carved and pegged (the club left as a trademark, unwhittled)—an oaken frame somehow assaulted. I am cramped, unable to move . . .

> *Moby-Dick:* "*For not only are whalemen as a body unexempt from that ignorance and superstitiousness hereditary to all sailors; but of all sailors, they are by all odds the most directly brought into contact with whatever is appallingly astonishing in the sea; face to face they not only eye its greatest marvels, but, hand to jaw, give battle to them. Alone, in such remotest waters, that though you sailed a thousand miles, and passed a thousand shores, you would not come to any chiselled hearthstone, or aught hospitable beneath that part of the sun; in such latitudes and longitudes, pursuing too such a calling as he does, the whaleman is wrapped by influences all tending to make his fancy pregnant with many a mighty birth.*"

> "*But far beneath this wondrous world upon the surface, another and still stranger world met our eyes as we gazed over the side. For, suspended in those watery vaults, floated the forms of the nursing mothers of the whales, and those that by their enormous girth seemed shortly to become mothers.*"

> "*One of those little infants, that from certain queer tokens seemed hardly a day old, might have measured some fourteen feet in length, and some six feet in girth. He was a little frisky; though as yet his body seemed scarce yet recovered from that irksome position it had so lately occupied . . . where, tail to head, and all ready for the final spring, the unborn whale lies bent like a Tartar's bow.*"

Sitting cramped, I recall the maternity hospital where, three times, I have taken Linda to produce: the old building, crowded and outdated; the various corridors leading, like the spokes of a wheel, to the hub, the labor and delivery rooms—corridors filled with grunting, sweating and sometimes screaming women; the labor room itself often hurriedly converted for a delivery—the building charged with haste and effort to cope with the mighty postwar tide of infants, rushing down the corridors, thrusting into the world.

Again, I am assaulted, the sensation this time largely in my head.

There is a sense of separation, the skull, like a case, holding firm under attack, and the brains, separate, trapped within—struggling and pushing . . . I attempt to scream, but the action of throat muscles, as of all else, is suspended, and I am left with silence . . .

> (*Melville, describing the pyramids: "A feeling of awe & terror came over me. Dread of the Arabs. Offering to lead me into a side-hole. The Dust. Long arched way,—then down as in a coal shaft. Then as in mines, under the sea. (At one moment seeming in the Mammoth Cave. Subterranean gorges, &c.) The stooping & doubling . . ."*

Thrusting my body back full length in the chair, I try to break the enclosure, the cramp—but there is no change: each position, each arrangement of trunk, head and limbs, becomes ultimate, a final one, from which my frame would become a thing made, without life.

Shifting again, unable to create Space, I try to reach with awareness alone, to grasp and control Time . . . and am reminded at once of childhood, when I slipped and fell into the post-hole: alone at the end of the corn field, with earth all around me, rising to beyond the top of my head—there is again the dizziness, the volatile awareness, expanding in proportion to my confinement, and the loneliness, the waiting . . .

> <u>Moby-Dick</u>: *"Leaning over in his hammock, Queequeg long regarded the coffin with an attentive eye. He then called for his harpoon, had the wooden stock drawn from it, and then had the iron part placed in the coffin along with one of the paddles of his boat. All by his own request, also, biscuits were then ranged around the sides within: a flask of fresh water was placed at the head, and a small bag of woody earth scraped up in the hold at the foot; and a piece of sail cloth being rolled up for a pillow, Queequeg now entreated to be lifted into his final bed, that he might make trial of its comforts, if any it had. He lay without moving a few minutes, then told one to go to his bag and bring out his little god, Yojo. Then crossing his arms on his breast with Yojo between, he called for the coffin lid (hatch he called it) to be placed over him. The head part turned over with a leather hinge, and there lay Queequeg in his coffin with little but his composed countenance in view. 'Rarmai' (it will do; it is easy), he mur-*

mured at last, and signed to be replaced in his hammock."

and <u>Bartleby</u>: *"The yard was entirely quiet. It was not accessible to the common prisoners. The surrounding walls, of amazing thickness, kept off all sounds behind them. The Egyptian character of the masonry weighed upon me with its gloom. But a soft imprisoned turf grew underfoot. The heart of the eternal pyramids, it seemed, wherein by some strange magic, through the clefts grass seed, dropped by birds, had sprung.*

"Strangely huddled at the base of the wall—his knees drawn up, and lying on his side, his head touching the cold stones—I saw the wasted Bartleby. But nothing stirred. I paused; then went close up to him; stooped over, and saw that his dim eyes were open; otherwise he seemed profoundly sleeping. Something prompted me to touch him. I felt his hand, when a tingling shiver ran up my arm and down my spine . . ."

and there was Navidad: first toe-hold, first bit of land secured and colonized, in the New World: the inhabitants, to a man, wiped out . . .

Waiting now, the very quality of it sinking in me, so that waiting becomes a kind of desperation, hopelessness, I remain huddled, cramped and desolate, as though dead . . .

T W O

Homer, <u>The Odyssey</u>: **". . . a sea broke over him with such terrific fury that the raft reeled again, and he was carried overboard a long way off. He let go the helm, and the force of the hurricane was so great that it broke the mast half way up, and both sail and yard went over into the sea. For a long time Ulysses was under water, and it was all he could do to rise to the surface again . . ."**

and Leucothea, marine goddess, white goddess, **". . . rising like a seagull from the waves, took her seat upon the raft . . ."** and spoke to Ulysses:

"'... strip, leave your raft to drive before the wind, and swim to the Phaeacian coast where better luck awaits you. And here, take my veil and put it around your chest; it is enchanted, and you can come to no harm so long as you wear it. As soon as you touch land, throw it back as far as you can into the sea, and then go away again.' With these words she took off her veil and gave it to him. Then she dived down again like a sea-gull and vanished beneath the dark blue waters."

An enchanted veil . . .

(The medical book:

("It is inferred that the human embryo . . . forms an amnion cavity in its solid ectodermal mass."

("If the tough amnion fails to burst, the head is delivered enveloped in it and it is then known popularly as the 'caul'."

The caul—an enchanted veil—presumed to bring luck, to prevent shipwreck, and save from drowning . . .

(there was the one advertized in the London Times—May 8, 1848—the owner asking 6 guineas, the caul "having been afloat with its last owner forty years, through all the perils of a seaman's life, and the owner died at last in his bed, at the place of his birth."

The pressure is growing, and my body, pushed tight against it, is now immovable; tremendous effort is exerted, at every point and plane of skin surface, to maintain the contact, and therefore any hope of identity. My skull, where the tension becomes greatest, is a fragile vault, in which I swim, helpless, as in an ocean.

I am aware of the clubfoot, of the five toes, and the flesh fusing them...

(the medical book:

("Syndactylism: . . . a common cause is adhesions of the fetus to the amnion."

There is an explosion, detonating somewhere in my head, and spreading with force and violence. The pressure collapses, and all sense of balance is gone, leaving me dizzy and ill. It is like shipwreck in a storm, the ship broken and scattered, the timbers—timbers of my skull—crashing against one another in gigantic waves. The structure—the partition between left and right sides in my head—is shattered, so that there is no longer an origin of direction, of motion, and I drift randomly, without form or shape . . .

> (*Moby-Dick:* "*. . . the breaking-up of the ice-bound stream of Time.*"
>
> *and* Cosmology: *"For then . . . we see that . . . all the nebulae were packed into a small region . . . years ago and moved away as though an explosion had taken place there, each with its own individual velocity . . ."*
> *". . . for an infinite period in the distant past there was a completely homogeneous distribution of matter in equilibrium . . . until some event started off the expansion, which has been going on at an increasing pace ever since."*

At the zero point of creation, when all is infinite mass and zero size . . . from this point—to one second—the distribution of elements occurs . . .

Gaseous Nebulae, coalescing into small suns, the suns clustering into galaxies,

The galaxies swirling, with angular momentum, in vortices,

> (like a hand swirled in water,
>
> (or like dust motes in an ever-expanding balloon . . .

particles in vortices,

sub-particles in vortices,

planets . . .

My body, huddled before a makeshift desk—an old door lain flat on crates—is relinquished, abandoned . . .

floating above it, above the ancient house and attic, above Indiana and the broad continent, I am no longer Michael, but have become everyone . . . no longer compact with pain, fear, anger and contentment, I am only aware . . .

aware of explosion and outflow, of letting go and spreading apart, of vaporizing into widening space . . .

> (*Cosmology: "In many ways we consider radiative energy to be 'lost' energy, picturing somehow space as an infinite receptacle, an almost perfect sink."*

No longer Michael, I am without borders . . . I glance down and see the city, the suburban row houses, hanging by television aerials from the atmosphere . . .

Turning from these, I drift, further and further from the land . . .

> (*Melville, in Pierre: "Better might one be pushed off into the material spaces beyond the uttermost orbit of our sun, than once feel himself fairly afloat in himself!"*

Once again, I lose depth perception; the world beneath me, and the stars, are flat, without dimension. Further, I am unable to see through the centre of the eye, the images reaching me only peripherally . . . I see only through the white. I am floating in space, without center or distance . . .

> (*Kinematic Relativity: "Here it is sufficient to recall that 'space' is not a physical attribute of the universe, but is a mode of description of phenomena which is at the disposal of the observer . . ."*

Everything comes to me in gray, a perfect gray, perfect in its neatness: tiny dots, as though created by a pointillist, ranging from black through various grays to white. I might be peering at a movie or television screen, or, perhaps, through Mike Jr.'s space helmet . . . or the gray gauze of a churchman's eyes:

a membrane, imperfectly transparent, filtering and veiling all reality...

I find my hands, clenched like a baby's, rubbing clumsily at my cheeks, eyes, forehead . . .

> (the root of the word caul is the same as that for hell and cellar: a matter of hiding . . .

All at once, my fists hang away from my face. The gray, peripheral images vanish, and are replaced by an unvarying white . . .

> *Moby-Dick:* "*. . . there yet lurks an elusive something in the in-nermost idea of this hue, which strikes more of panic to the soul than that redness which affrights in blood.*
>
> "*This elusive quality it is, which causes the thought of white-ness, when divorced from more kindly associations, and coupled with any object terrible in itself, to heighten that terror to the furthest bounds. Witness the white bear of the poles, and the white shark of the tropics; what but their smooth, flaky whiteness makes them the transcendent horrors they are? That ghastly whiteness it is which imparts such an abhorrent mildness, even more loathsome than terrific, to the dumb bloating of their aspect.*"
>
> "*What is it that in the Albino man so peculiarly repels and often shocks the eye, as that sometimes he is loathed by his own kith and kin! It is that whiteness that invests him, a thing ex-pressed by the name he bears. The Albino is as well made as other men—has no substantive deformity—and yet this mere aspect of all pervading whiteness makes him more strangely hideous than the ugliest abortion. Why should this be so?*"
>
> "*Nor, in some things, does the common, hereditary experience of all mankind fail to bear witness to the supernaturalism of this hue. It cannot well be doubted, that the one visible quality in the aspect of the dead which most appals the gazer, is the marble pallor lingering there . . .*"
>
> *Melville's bedroom, described by his granddaughter:* "*The great mahogany desk, heavily bearing up four shelves of dull gilt and leather books; the high dim book-case . . . ; the small black iron bed, covered with dark cretonne; the narrow iron grate . . .*"
>
> *and Lizzie's:* "*That was a very different place—sunny, com-fortable and familiar, with a sewing machine and a white bed like other people's.*"
>
> *Olson, describing Melville:* "*He made a white marriage.*"

> (but before that, before Lizzie, before the white, there was Fayaway, dark, on a green island . . .

I recall the many hospitals I have visited, studied and worked in: the floors, walls and furniture in pastels, the colors, the force of color, bleached out of them; the apparatus of laboratory, surgery and kitchen in chrome and steel; and everything else, whether intimately or remotely pertaining to healing—the uniforms of nurse, intern, attendant and doctor, the sheets covering the sick and the ceilings over the beds, the curtains, screens, towels and bandages—all drained and blanched, sterile and antiseptic—all white.

and there was Melville, possessed—like Ahab—by that "dark Hindoo half of nature"—and to all who surrounded him—to Lizzie, to his sons and daughters, to the Gansevoorts and Melvilles—a poison, potent and to be feared . . .

a sepsis.

White and vague, I am drifting, without space or time . . .

> (*Cosmology: ". . . since the age of the universe (especially if its origin was catastrophic) cannot be less than the age of any part of it, however small."*

. . . disincarnate . . .

> (*Melville: "While there is life hereafter, there is despair . . ."*

Once again, the tiny dots of gray appear, shaping images of Indiana, like the first image of the afternoon projected on a movie screen. I see the row houses, the factories and stores of Indianapolis, all neatly arranged and harmonized, a uniform gray . . .

. . . a vision of reality, filtered and orderly . . .

as an old sailor, retired ashore, makes a ship inside a bottle . . .

or a man makes a philosophy: life viewed through a caul.

I remember, in the psychiatric courses I took, studying the life of Freud, and discovering that the Viennese, father of modern psychology —the first to introduce modern man to the pear-shaped world from which he sprang—Freud was born with a caul . . .

Fusing with the amnion, becoming the amnion, turning all to gray and white, I am no longer Michael, but everyone—a particle in an explosion—all time and space—and therefore, nothing . . .

(Columbus: "The pilots. . . do not know the way to return thither . . . ; they would be obliged to go on a voyage of discovery as much as if they had never been there before. There is a mode of reckoning derived from astronomy which is sure and safe, and a sufficient guide to any one who understands it. This resembles a prophetic vision."

I look down at Michael, fixed in the chair—as the attic is fixed upon the house and the old house rooted in the soil—and the images suddenly vanish, whirling into one another. There is a different sensation —as though I had become sensitive to the spinning of the globe. I am aware again of my body, and feel myself sucked down, drawn into it. Within my skull all is gray chaos, whirling and dizzy, with no origin of direction or motion. The desk, the attic, the world are pitching and rolling, and I am ill . . .

. . . drawn into the body, I am drawn down with it: compacted and chaotic, beyond control, I begin strangely to move . . . I seem drowning, drawn to unknown bottoms . . . there is a monstrous, choking fear . . .

The medical book: "The amnion in the human develops probably by degeneration of the central portion of a lenticular enlargement of the cell mass . . ."

". . . but this has not yet been determined, even though of great significance in the production of monsters."

T H R E E

Melville, Benito Cereno: ". . . when at sunrise, the deponent coming on deck, the negro Babo showed him a skeleton, which had been substituted for the ship's proper figure-head . . ."

. . . the proper and original figurehead having been that of the discoverer, Christopher Columbus.

Thus Melville, after Moby-Dick, after the sinking of the Pequod—sucked into the whirlpool, at the very bottom—yields the overwater discoverer . . . and

"Seguid vuestro jefe" . . . the leader, in this case, a skeleton . . .
My left leg—lying straight from the edge of the chair to the floor beneath the desk—seems to enlarge, the flesh prickly and fat . . . then it goes numb: all sensation vanishes . . .

and it occurs to me that, whereas in Moby-Dick Melville fought his way upstream, like the Pacific salmon, to the original sources—in Pierre, there was no need to return, no stream to ascend . . . the fight gone out of him, he remained still, and the past overwhelmed him . . . sinking, drowning, he pulled the world, his family, in over himself . . .

. . . the amniotic waters, closing over the eye of the vortex, over Melville's wreck . . .

Although in Moby-Dick Melville reached deep into "the invisible spheres . . . formed in fright," he yet maintained freeboard, working from above the surface—if safe by only the few perilous inches of a whaleboat . . . but in Pierre, the author, the story, the people of whom he wrote, all are one—gelatinous, sub-aquatic—the verbs become blobs of sound . . .

The absence of sensation in my left leg has become something positive, and yet I can't put words to it . . . the leg having passed into a condition remote from the rest of my body, untranslatable . . . I am aware only of its motionlessness, of its arrest not only in space but in time . . . being stopped itself, the leg stops the rest of me: my body stiffens, tenses, for or against what, I cannot tell

. . . a thought floats in, however, that I am struggling, by physical force, to prevent Melville from writing Pierre . . .

> *"For while still dreading your doom, you foreknow it. Yet how foreknow and dread in one breath . . . ?"*
>
> *Thus, Pierre. And Melville—as Ahab, barely before the sinking of the Pequod—foreknew his doom: ". . . from all your furthest bounds, pour ye now in, ye bold billows of my whole foregone life . . . !"*

I remember Carl, in St. Louis, after the war, after he had come back from nineteen months in a Japanese Prisoner-Of-War Camp: we were afraid of what had happened to his mind, and, for want of a better answer, I was trying to get him to a psychiatrist, to help him go over his experiences, untangle something of what he was, what had happened to him . . . I recall the look on his face when I made the suggestion: the features withdrawing, not from me, but from one another, shifting their arrangement, becoming without form; and the smile, part of his mouth spreading, as he said, "I ain't drowning, Mike boy . . ."

My leg is now dead, passed into a condition from which there is no recall. I become aware of the hip joint, the part that is still me. I cherish the separation, the feeling of identity going no further than the hip . . .

Ahab: ". . . it was Moby-Dick that dismasted me . . ."

Moby-Dick . . . a great white monster, with "a hump like a snow-hill . . ."

not Leucothea, not a white and winged goddess, protectress, who gave Ulysses an enchanted veil . . .

but moving out from this, from the closed and friendly Mediterranean, from the near ocean shores,

moving out, as Columbus, across the Atlantic, and, through Melville, into the Pacific:

the white gull become a white whale, cast in monstrous, malignant revenge . . .

Melville, in the Pacific—the western extreme of American force—untethered, fatherless, the paternity blasted—turning—as Ahab—with vengeance and malice to match the monster's: turning and thrusting back to his own beginnings: to

Moby-Dick, the white monster: to Maria Gansevoort Melville . . .

> (*Lizzie's account of Herman: "A severe attack of what he called crick in the back laid him up at his Mothers in Gansevoort in March 1858—and he never regained his former vigor & strength."*)

The snow-hill hump, rumbling in the interior caverns of the sea book, bursts forth as the ultimate image in the book of the drowned—all of

<u>Pierre</u> perhaps being written as an excuse to expose it:

> *"'. . . in thy breasts, life for infants lodgeth not, but death-milk for thee and me!—The drug!' and tearing her bosom loose, he seized the secret vial nestling there."*

Carl, some years ago, on one of his rare and random splurges of reading—invading the library, chewing his way through stacks of books—came up with a volume of Indian legends: there was one about a woman with a toothed vagina, who had killed many men by having intercourse with them—but the hero inserted sticks too hard for her to masticate, and thus knocked out the teeth . . . and there was another about the first woman in the world, whose vagina contained a carnivorous fish . . .

> (Columbus, in the <u>Boca de la Sierpe</u>—mouth of the serpent—observed that the tides were much greater than anywhere else in the Indies, the current roaring like surf . . .

Dead-legged, helpless and unwilling, I feel my body dragged down . . .

> *Melville, blubbering from beneath the ocean, announces <u>Pierre</u> to a Hawthorne—not Nathaniel, but Sophia: "My Dear Lady, I shall not again send you a bowl of salt water. The next chalice I shall commend, will be a rural bowl of milk."*

> *From a contemporary review of <u>Pierre</u>: "The sooner this author is put in a ward the better."*

F O U R

The interior of my head is an ocean, vast and unvarying, the watery horizon curving as with the curve of the globe. There is no island, no source of direction, or action. Floating, centerless, in this expanse, I am ready to drown . . .

But there is a sudden change: my left leg—or that which had been my left leg—comes back to me: I feel blood and warmth entering again, sweeping in waves from the hip, and with this, the rest of me, all of my body becomes charged with sensation . . .

There is also a difference: sinking in one ocean, I have risen to the surface of another—in a different hemisphere, or on the other side of the equator. The heart beats, the blood flows, the lungs inhale and discharge air—but all are radically altered. Reaching for the butt of the cigar resting in the ash tray, I am surprised to discover the gesture originating, not in my right hand, but in my left. My arm and shoulder, my whole left side, ache and feel uncomfortable—but this is not so strange as when I try to countermand the order, originate the gesture as I would normally, from the right. Plunging once more into the ocean, I attempt to force myself back, to force the gesture, and all gestures, to emerge and spring from the right: my body becomes rigid, all the machinery, all the moving parts, jammed . . .

> *Pierre:* "*. . . a sudden, unwonted, and all-pervading sensation seized him. He knew not where he was; he did not have any ordinary life-feeling at all. He could not see; though instinctively putting his hand to his eyes, he seemed to feel that the lids were open. Then he was sensible of a combined blindness, and vertigo, and staggering; before his eyes a million green meteors danced; he felt his foot tottering on the curb, he put out his hands, and knew no more for the time. When he came to himself he found that he was lying crosswise in the gutter, dabbled with mud and slime. He raised himself to try if he could stand; but the fit was entirely gone.*"
>
> *and Murray, commenting on this:* "*Although there is no record of Melville's having suffered an attack of syncope, there is verisimilitude in his description of Pierre's fainting. Furthermore, the time relation of Pierre's attack . . . would indicate that Melville himself had experienced syncope.*"

> > (From the medical book: ". . . characterized by an abrupt onset, with uneasiness, weakness, restlessness, vague abdominal discomfort associated with moderate nausea, lightheadedness, blurring of vision, inability to walk, cold perspiration, collapse, unconsciousness, and sometimes a flaccid paralysis and mild convulsions . . .")

Melville, standing on a Pacific island—Typee—floating up to effervescent <u>Mardi</u>—charging, then, full force, back to the origin and beginning of things—the center of the whale-herd, east of the Straits of Sunda—and turning, to plunge . . .

> (*from a letter, written before <u>Moby-Dick</u>: "I love all men who <u>dive</u>. Any fish can swim near the surface, but it takes a great whale to go down stairs five miles or more . . ."*

. . . plunge to the depths and bottom of the ocean, to drown, as <u>Pierre</u> . . .

rising, then, struggling to disgorge the ocean from his lungs (and his head), to find another island, another origin of action,

through syncope: fainting—a small and imitation death—perhaps a drowning . . . in effect, saying to himself—and to any who would listen:

"I have to change centers, and I have to drown to do it."

Failed as an author—and as a Pittsfield farmer—failing now in health, to the extent that the family had him examined by Dr. Holmes in regard to his sanity—Melville set about in his own way to recenter: he took to writing verse . . .

> "*For poetry is not a thing of ink and rhyme, but of thought and act . . .*" (*Melville*)

The joints, the motion-sources of my body remain rigid, the bones and muscles forcing against one another. My tongue and eyelids are heavy, and

I recall a time when Carl came home for a visit—it was just before the war, and I was away in medical school: he was experiencing mysterious convulsions, and the doctors for some time withheld a diagnosis, uncertain of what term to use—although I knew they suspected a recurrence of hydrocephalus. Mother and I were subjected to the electroencephalograph, in search of genetic dysrhythmia—but the findings were negative. Carl experienced all the typical preconvulsive phenomena—unexplained faints, attacks of giddiness, sleepiness, myoclonic jerks—and finally the diagnosis was made: acquired epilepsy . . .

> (the word meaning to "seize upon": as a drowning man would seize upon an island . . .

Perhaps because I was studying medicine—and was, as well, his brother—Carl sent me reports on his seizures . . . fragmentary letters, notes jotted on old pieces of wrapping paper, or the backs of prescriptions:

"A touch of fear . . . great thickness and heaviness, moving to my tongue . . . last stage before the attack.

"This time the aura was black, and the closing-in type . . .

"It is always flashover, definite—like the stepping out of a warm room into the cold . . .

"Have discovered I can induce the aura: driving the car, I put myself as someone in one of the other cars, then someone in another car, then another, and so forth—an overwhelmed-by-numbers bizzniss turns up, and right under (or after) that: the aura . . .

". . . a breeze . . . gateway to a fabulous world, everything maneuverable . . . like an explosion, reaching, spreading into widening space, all white . . .

"As for question of the head and interpenetration . . . the effect is gradual . . . as for shape, configuration, the same, but as for size, I don't know . . .

"While I write this, I feel the approach of the aura. Realize that I have walked past where it is stored . . . go back and contact it . . . now it has me, full force . . . as long as I keep my eyes closed, it's there . . . Feeling: it's all in my head, and I'm in and occupy very little of it . . . all the world in there (or here) since my head is the limit of the world . . . I am a little bigger than the rest of the universe . . . the feeling now persists even with eyes open: I make desperate efforts to get away from it . . .

"Thought, under attack: I must recap the birth of the universe . . ."

(from the medical book: "A patient who invariably dislocated his right shoulder as he fell, explained this by saying that he would see a star before him for which he would reach . . .")

and Carl: "A dream: conjure up a chorus, with the director

116

(thin-faced) telling them to start the theme, god damnit, on the UP beat! Chorus furious, marches on him, on the strong beat . . . feeling of horror . . ."

(the medical book: "The authors present the case of a woman aged 44 in whom extensive clinical investigation failed to reveal an acquired cerebral lesion, but which represented a case of musicogenic epilepsy. The patient experienced increases of blood pressure, heart rate, and respiration while listening to music. Fits could not be induced by pure tones, although the patient felt emotional to a tone of 512 cycles which persisted and was varied in loudness. Different kinds of music were invariably followed by a fit within five minutes."

The period in which Carl had attacks lasted only a few months, terminating as abruptly as it started; and for this, the doctors had no explanation. Nor would Carl himself speak of it, then or thereafter . . .

Melville, collapsing the world of Pittsfield and the Pacific, salvaged the remains, hoarded them into 104 East 26th Street—fortunate to be taken on as outdoor customs inspector (badge #75), Port of New York, at a reward of $4 per diem (later reduced to $3.60). Reduced, circumscribed, and ageing, he still thrashed . . .

From Daniel Orme (and perhaps he meant Daniel Or Me): " . . . his moodiness and mutterings, his strange freaks, starts, eccentric shrugs and grimaces . . ."

and from a contemporary review of Melville's verse: "Mr. Melville has abundant force and fire . . . But he has written too rapidly to avoid great crudities. His poetry runs into the epileptic. His rhymes are fearful . . ."

F I V E

Moby-Dick: "But now that he had apparently made every preparation for death; now that his coffin was proved a good fit, Queequeg suddenly rallied; soon there seemed no need of the carpenter's

117

> box: and thereupon, when some expressed their delighted sur-
> prise, he, in substance, said, that the cause of his sudden con-
> valescence was this;—at a critical moment, he had just recalled a
> little duty ashore, which he was leaving undone; and therefore had
> changed his mind about dying: he could not die yet, he averred.
> They asked him, then, whether to live or die was a matter of his
> own sovereign will and pleasure. He answered, certainly. In a
> word, it was Queequeg's conceit, that if a man made up his mind
> to live, mere sickness could not kill him: nothing but a whale, or
> a gale, or some violent, ungovernable, unintelligent destroyer of
> that sort."

I experience an abrupt relaxation, a lifting of tensions, and, with this, a restoration of vision, so marked, the dark corners and recesses of the attic stand out so sharply—that I seem to have gained new powers. Random motives, impulses to shift and rearrange limbs and muscles, occur throughout my frame. I am restless, moving, wanting to move in ways I have never tried before . . .

> Melville: "Let us speak, tho' we show all our faults and weak-
> nesses,—for it is a sign of strength to be weak, to know it, and
> out with it . . ."

Reviving within myself, I am aware also of external motion, motion of my body as a whole, from the outside, and there are the two: inside and outside, working with and against one another . . .

Stretched loosely in the chair, giving the sensations full play, I am aware of fresh sources of energy opening in me, opening barely in time to be poured into the increasing demands, both in action and duration, that are to be made upon me . . .

> Melville, after _Moby-Dick_: "Lord, when shall we be done grow-
> ing? As long as we have anything more to do, we have done
> nothing."

> and Las Casas, describing Christopher, embarking on the third
> voyage: ". . . wherefore it appeared to him that what he already
> had done was not sufficient but that he must renew his labors . . ."

I remember the three occasions—but especially the first—of Linda's pregnancies . . . our watching and wondering, as the end of her term approached, what day or night it would be when we would hurry to the hospital . . . the obvious pleasure with which she allowed me to place my hand on her, to try to anticipate, as husband, father, and doctor, the exact hour . . . her figure, short and broad, so exquisitely designed for childbirth, carrying the weight lower and lower, as the head approached the cervix, the ultimate part of its pear-shaped world, until it seemed that the infant must drop at any moment—in the kitchen, the bathroom, or on the bed where he began . . .

> *Columbus: ". . . it is impossible to give a correct account of all our movements, because I was carried away by the current so many days without seeing land."*
>
> *and from the "Libretto": ". . . not very far from there they found a stream of water from east to west, so swift and impetuous that the Admiral says that never since he has sailed . . . has he been more afraid."*

I am shaken—head, ribs and limbs—by a tremendous effort . . .

> *Columbus: "At this time the river forced a channel for itself, by which I managed, with great difficulty, to extricate . . ."*
>
> *and Las Casas: "Arriving at the said mouth . . . he found a great struggle between the fresh water striving to go out to the sea and the salt water of the sea striving to enter the gulf, and it was so strong and fearful, that it raised a great swell, like a very high hill, and with this, both waters made a noise and thundering, from east to west, very great and fearful, with currents of water, and after one came four great waves one after the other, which made contending currents; here they thought to perish . . ."*
>
> *"It pleased the goodness of God that from the same danger safely and deliverance came to them and the current of the fresh water overcame the current of the salt water and carried the ships safely out, and thus they were placed in security; because when God wills that one or many shall be kept alive, water is a remedy for them."*

The Odyssey: "Here at last Ulysses' knees and strong hands failed him, for the sea had completely broken him. His body was all swollen, and his mouth and nostrils ran down like a river with sea-water, so that he could neither breathe nor speak, and lay swooning from near exhaustion; presently, when he had got his breath and came to himself again, he took off the scarf that Leucothea had given him and threw it

back into the salt stream of the river, whereon Leucothea received it into her hands from the wave that bore it towards her. Then he left the river, laid himself down among the rushes, and kissed the bounteous earth."

I am invaded by a great warmth, my entire skin surface tingling . . .

(Melville: ". . . as we mortals ourselves spring all naked and scabbardless into the world."

. . . and with it, an indescribable relief, satisfaction and well-being. Reaching for the cigar butt, I lean back, stretch my legs, and light up again, relishing the warmth of the match flame, as it nearly burns my face. Drawing lungs full of smoke, I tilt my head against the back of the chair, and watch the clouds, floating in the yellow lamplight to the rafters. I recall the cigars I smoked and gave away at the plant on the occasions of Mike Jr.'s birth, our first born; and, with the tobacco smoke, I taste again the pleasure, the pride that I enjoyed at that time —pride such as a man might feel at the mouth of the Mississippi or Amazon, sharing in those waters that push back the ocean, the waters they are in the act of joining . . .

BATTLE PIECES
AND ASPECTS OF THE WAR

ONE

"**I**T was on a bomber run that Rico and I cracked up near a hospital in China—a small outpost hospital—and discovered that Concha was assigned to it. Christ, we didn't even know she was out of the states . . .

"We bailed out and no one was hurt except Rico, who had stayed behind to shoot out the bombsight and set the ship afire. He tore a shoulder pretty bad, but he clamped the cut himself. By twos and threes the Chinese took us to the hospital, where they assured us Concha would smuggle us back to HQ. Seems she'd been doing this for months . . .

"We arrived at the same time the Japs captured the hospital and surrounding town. Rico had cautioned us before we bailed out to destroy our insignia and not to admit to being officers, so the Japs would think us privates and not try to pump us. However, the Japs seem to base seniority on age, so Rico and I, not being in our twenties, were stuck—as well as a fifty-year-old sergeant, who they thought must be a general: he was tortured, and when he wouldn't talk—because he didn't know anything—they cut his head off, to scare the rest of us.

"Rico raged and cursed when he was tortured, but appeared more angry than hurt. I wish I could say as much for myself . . .

"Concha, I guess, didn't know what to expect . . . she was only thinking of her patients. This was a general hospital, and among other things she had women in labor, and some who had

121

just delivered. The Japs explained, through a Chinese doctor, that they were going to take over the hospital for billets . . .

"They started evacuating the patients at sword point. One of the privates threw a baby up and caught it through the belly on his bayonet; Concha didn't move, but when the C. O. laughed, she lost her head and struck him. It wasn't a ladylike slap, but, well, you know Concha—she just lifted one off the floor and planted it on him, and he went down for the count. It was beautiful . . . but we all knew she would suffer for it. At his command, they grabbed her, yanked her back and forth among them, until we couldn't always keep sight of her. When the crowd thinned out she was naked, her skin in ribbons, her long hair hanging down—and several handfuls trailed from many hands. Her knuckles were bleeding, her eyes flashed, her head was up and she was mad clear through. I was proud of her. She had given a good account, too, being outnumbered—had blacked several eyes, and quite a few men had lumps appearing on their jaws.

"The Chinese doctor groaned aloud when he heard the C. O. say that he would rape her first, and then the others could have her. He explained that she was in for a bad time, she was such a small woman . . .

"We were invited to watch, with our hands tied behind our backs. They threw her to the ground and when they twisted her legs behind her shoulders, and her hips came out of joint or broke, Rico yelled curses and tore at his bonds until his wrists were bleeding. The officer, of course, couldn't get into her and he seemed to be in a hurry. He gave a command and a soldier jammed his rifle barrel into her three or four times until he broke through . . . She blacked out at the first jab . . .

"He raped her then . . . some of us declined the invitation to look and closed our eyes and turned our heads—but they went around our circle and cut off a few pairs of eyelids."

> **(Moby-Dick: "That unblinkingly vivid Japanese sun . . ."**

Carl . . . from notes made during and after his captivity, and secreted in his duffle, until finally, in a backhanded gesture—placing them where I and no one else would discover them—he let them fall into my hands.

Early in the war, he had tried to enlist in the Air Force, but, for some reason, had been turned down. Cabling Rico—the only survivor of the Spanish brothers—in Havana, he arranged to meet him in England: he assumed the pose of some sort of civilian technician, and managed to hitchhike on military craft, in a matter of only a few hours, from Indianapolis to London. Together, Carl and Rico enlisted in the RAF.

For months we heard nothing—until a card came from Concha: she was trying to trace Rico through Carl, and Carl through me. I didn't know until years after, when I read Carl's notes, that, with my reply, she had headed for London, and, with her medical training—she had specialized in surgery—had been taken into the British Army, and given an assignment in China.

There others who made notes—the Chinese doctor, Concha's adjutant, was one—and these I found with Carl's:

> *"I once asked Concha where she had gained her knowledge and technique in gunshot wounds (she was too young for the first war) and she told me that she had had ample experience during the various revolutions in Cuba. (In one of these, her father and twin brothers were army officers, and she fought with the students against them—as I believe she fought against her father in Spain. When her father and Rico's twin were killed, she may have suffered more than any of us realize . . .*
>
> *"Her surgery was remarkable, I've never seen anyone, even a man, more deft and sure. Her reactions were quick, her decisions rapid and accurate, her reflexes amazing. The Japs have ruined her hands, they now shake badly . . .*
>
> *"Our captors could never be still for long; they chose projects and then suddenly dropped them for no apparent reason. When they attacked Carl, though, they stayed with the idea until it is a miracle he wasn't killed. They fought over him, dragged him around by his hair (his hands were bound together over his head) and all the time the whip never ceased lashing his back. His mouth was bleeding; blood came from his nose in spurts and bubbles. His knees were raw from being dragged back and forth over the sand and gravel; when one tired of the whip, another took over. They broke his teeth and ribs, and when he evacuated, they*

dragged him about in it. His pleading was pitiful, it was what might have been expected from a woman, in extreme pain and fear . . .

"When finally they tired of him, only Rico and I would touch him—the others turned away. We tried to clean him as best we could, but we had nothing to work with. Rico got some putrid water from a ditch, and we threw it over his buttocks. He was in a great deal of pain for some time—broken teeth and ribs, abrasions on his legs, his back practically flayed. And all the time he tried to explain himself, weeping and pleading incoherently. I don't know what I pitied more, his condition of mind or body. He finally fell into an exhausted sleep. I think Rico was disgusted with him, but he has a big heart and like me was more charitable, because we felt pity at having had to watch—and we were forced to watch. Neither of us, after all, knew how we would react in his position. The Japs are past masters at reducing human beings . . ."

(Melville—1850—admits the East on board:

"With a start all glared at dark Ahab, who was surrounded by five dusky phantoms that seemed fresh formed out of air."

"For me, I silently recalled the mysterious shadows I had seen creeping on board the Pequod during the dim Nantucket dawn . . ."

". . . while the subordinate phantoms soon found their place among the crew, though still as it were somehow distinct from them, yet that hair-turbaned Fedallah remained a muffled mystery to the last . . . He was such a creature as civilized, domestic people in the temperate zone only see in their dreams, and that but dimly; but the like of whom now and then glide among the unchanging Asiatic communities, especially the Oriental isles to the east of the continent—those insulated, immemorial, unalterable countries, which even in these modern days, still preserve much of the ghostly aboriginalness of earth's primal generations . . ."

Carl:

"There was one tree in the yard and in it they hung by the wrists the women who were about to deliver; they tied strips of sheets

between their legs, and left them hanging until they died. Those whose kids they had murdered just wandered around crying while their breasts swelled with milk, until some of them burst.

"They gave us nothing to drink and we were fed only salt pork, fish heads and rice."

(Columbus—who had set out in search of Cipango—sends a message back to the Sovereigns:

> ". . . the greatest necessity we feel here at the present time is for wines and it is what we desire most to have . . . It is necessary that each time a caravel comes here, fresh meat shall be sent, and even more than that, lambs and little ewe lambs, more females than males, and some little yearling calves, male and female . . ."

Carl:

"Thirst became an agony, until one man went berserk and grabbed a Chinese woman and started sucking her breast. She screamed and fought at first, until she realized that the pressure in her breasts was being relieved, and in a moment each of us had a woman, or half of one . . .

"The Japs laughed and capered around . . . they weren't missing a trick. Mike, I wielded a whip on some of our own men, to save myself. I went down on my knees to those little brown bastards and did as they told me. I must have taken down a hundred of them . . ."

(Columbus:

> "Thus, as I have already said, I saw no cannibals, nor did I hear of any, except in a certain island called Charis, which is the second from Española, on the side towards India, where dwell a people who are considered by the neighboring islanders as most ferocious: and these feed upon human flesh."

(and elsewhere:

> "The boys that they take they castrate; as we cause castration; because they become fatter for eating; and the mature men also, when they take them they kill them and they eat them: and they eat the intestines fresh and the extreme members of the body . . ."

Carl:

"Believe me, Mike, it was the warm milk—the horror of those days and nights, and the affection I had for him. He had been

*through so much, and when they shot the aphrodisiac into him
and we heard what they intended, the Chinese doctor groaned
again.*

*"Night fell, and Rico had thrown his beaten body off Concha's a
hundred times, and each time they threw him on her he promised
her he wouldn't hurt her. She didn't appear to be afraid, even
when some of the boys shouted at him to take her, that he couldn't
fight that drug. He shook like the ague, and kept his jaws clamped
tight; his eyes burned, and he was so close to breaking that we all
wondered how he held out. The Japs finally tired of that game and
went inside for chow, and Rick stumbled off by himself . . .*

*"It was dark, and when I found him he was lying on his back,
his arms rigid at his sides, the bloody nail-less fingers clenched. I
ran my hands over his sweat-slick body . . .*

*"I had to hold his hips with both arms, he pitched so violently . . .
I could feel my mouth tearing and my jaws breaking . . ."*

(Ishmael, in <u>Moby-Dick</u>—embedded with a cannibal:

"I looked at the grand and glorious fellow . . ."

*"Wild he was; a very sight of sights to see; yet I began to feel
myself mysteriously drawn to him."*

*"For though I tried to move his arm—unlock his bridegroom
clasp—yet, sleeping as he was, he still hugged me tightly, as
though naught but death should part us . . ."*

(Melville, elsewhere:

> *"The Anglo-Saxons—lacking grace
> To win the love of any race;
> Hated by myriads dispossessed
> . . . —the Indians East and West."*

(and

> *"Asia shall stop her at the least,
> That old inertness of the East."*

Carl:

*"Did you ever see a man die, Mike? The Japs made me beat
Curley—one of our own boys—to death, and I guess that's when*

126

*I really lost my mind: I can't help it, it was a wonderful sensa-
tion . . . they had kicked in his face first, until we couldn't understand a word he said, but he pleaded and whimpered, and his
wild, pain-racked eyes stared at me . . .*

*"Among the prisoners was a missionary family, who had a little
girl about ten years old, fat, blue-eyed and blonde. The Japs
thought it would hurt the parents more if they tortured the child,
so they decided to rape her. They used a sword point to make her
big enough . . . Dozens of them took her . . . she lay in a pool of
blood, cried all the time, and never lost consciousness. We were
all driven crazy—I doubt if any one had ever said an unkind
word to her in her life, she just didn't know what it was all about.*

*"After chow the Japs came back and decided to have more game
with her. Rico didn't have a square inch of skin on him that
hadn't been torn or burned, and he couldn't get on his feet, but he
crawled over to her, spoke to her quietly, and put his hands—
burned and bleeding—on her neck. He put his head down on his
arms . . . and in seconds, she was dead. The Chinese doctor felt
her pulse, and then gently released Rico's hands . . .*

*"The Japs never could stand being frustrated, they almost killed
Rico for that gesture . . . I don't know how he survived it. Blood
trickled down his chin where he bit through his lip, and when
they left him, he shook uncontrollably . . ."*

T W O

When he was finally rescued—the town was relieved near the end of
the war—Carl didn't return directly to Indianapolis. Wealthy with
back pay, he went first to the Mayo Clinic, for plastic surgery and
other repairs; then he re-joined Rico and Concha, and two or three
others from the RAF—there was an ex-prizefighter, whose only name,
so far as I could find out, was Meat-Nose. They collected others—a
singer named Joey was one—and formed a dance band. One or two got
jobs as test pilots, on the side, and together they rented a ramshackle

old house on the coast of California, which they all shared.

Leaving Minnesota, Carl came first to Indianapolis, staying only overnight—his manner as affable, his personality and presence as broad, hazarded and infrangible as it had ever been. When I asked him once, only vaguely, about the war, he leaned back in his chair—I thought he would fall, or the chair would break; he laughed heartily, his great head rocking as I had seen it so often before—and changed the subject.

But he left his notes for me—though I didn't find them until later. I don't know how he did it—I was with him when he unpacked his duffle—saw him take out the dirty clothes, the spare airplane parts, pieces of sheet music, photographs of friends and bartenders; trinkets and lucky charms, Indian relics and archeological fragments; a thumbed and tattered collection of pre-war comic books—the circulating library of the POW camp; and, at the bottom of the sack, down among the last of the comics, a book that he must have picked up in England, published by John Lehman of London: Melville, H.: The Confidence Man.

Again, for a long time, we heard nothing. Then a letter came from Meat-Nose . . . he had heard that I was Carl's brother, and a doctor, and he was asking my help. He'd had a talk with Carl that he tape-recorded, without Carl knowing it, and he transcribed some of Carl's words and sent them to me:

> "*I don't expect you to understand, it's a feeling that can't be described. Joey is different . . . even after I'm through with him, the sensation of pleasure goes on and on and builds up until I'm drunk with it . . . nothing seems real, I'm above everything human, I see nothing but red streamers of blood widening out . . . For hours afterward I can see the kid's eyes wide with pain, his face twisted, and I can hear that voice everyone admires so beating in my ears, in my blood . . . after I'm home in bed, I can relive the whole thing . . .*
>
> "*I know he's insane. I wish I could stop. I never felt this way with anyone before. There have been others who were afraid of me, but none like Joe. When he's panicked to the edge of madness, I think my veins will bust . . .*
>
> "*When his voice is gone, and he can't manage to get on his knees*

without pulling himself up, I look at him, and I'm sad because he doesn't die. I tell him I hate him, I swear at him, and he tries to get to his knees and starts kissing my feet and looks at me with those wild eyes ... Even after I've thrown down the whip I like to sink my fingers into his flesh and twist it. He begs me to stop, prays to me, swears he wants to make me happy—then he says that if the only way I can love him is to hurt him, then hurt him more.

"What in hell keeps him alive? How does anyone survive ...? I thought sometimes that I'd reached the end with him, and I've even considered taking him away like he begs me to ... let his hair grow, dress him like a woman, take him where everyone will think he's my wife. I was about to make up my mind to do it, when he refused to let me cut him up so he'd look like a woman. Why in hell he wants to hang on to such a sorry mess of stuff as he has, I don't know, but the little bastard clings to it as though it were made of gold ..."

T H R E E

The cigar gone, burned down beyond re-kindling—the stump splayed in the ashtray—I close the books, and get to my feet. The suburbs, the city itself seem hushed ... standing alone at the desk, I enjoy for a moment possession of myself, and of the attic, the form and structure of the house, and beyond, the city, the plains.

My joints are stiff, and I recall the bottle of ale, drunk earlier in the evening, downstairs in the old kitchen, when I was in a nineteenth-century mood—a little painful now ...

The creak of the planks seems louder, as I move toward the stairs. Descending the dark stairwell, I tread softly.

The house is quiet, the lights out. Pausing a moment in the hallway, I can hear Linda's breathing. Then I pass down the second flight, and out the front door ...

The air is chilled, but the wind is quiet ... the blackberry winter, the catbird storm, subsiding as we push past midnight, into the early hours . . .

Returning to the kitchen, I think of eating—cold meat loaf, a piece of rye bread, another bottle of ale. There is an urge to turn on the television, hunt for some late show, a bit of fiction that will haul me into the screen, the eye of the thing. Hesitating between the two—refrigerator and TV—I am drawn both ways. Then I pass beyond them, move quietly to the stairs and climb again, both flights, moving swiftly through the dark, through the familiarity of many years in the old house. I climb once more to the attic.

FOUR

A card came from Carl, postmarked St. Louis. He said that he had left the coast for good, was in St. Louis, but gave no address.

Later I discovered that his departure, and the break-up of the band, was coincidental with the death, under mysterious circumstances, of the singer named Joey. Joey was a good sailor, had managed boats all his life—but he took a small catboat out when the storm warnings were up, headed the thing into the rain and wind . . . and, according to the Coast Guard, deliberately capsized her, turning downwind, and then coming about, so that she jibed. His body—what was left of it— was never found . . .

Why Carl came to St. Louis, in particular, I didn't know . . . although I found out later. I also found that he was not alone: he had brought Concha with him . . .

There followed a succession of weird illnesses, disconnected physical manifestations, and, as with the epilepsy, he took the trouble to report to me: random cards, postmarked St. Louis, giving the strict details, and no address.

He reported the appearance of a succession of shapes and markings in odd areas of his body—stars, crosses, and various abstractions, like microscopic cell life . . . One after another, or in groups, they appeared, and vanished . . .

*(Moby-Dick: ". . . the visible surface of the
Sperm Whale is not the least among the
many marvels he presents. Almost invariably it is all over obliquely crossed and re-
crossed with numberless straight marks in
thick array."*

*"By my retentive memory of the hiero-
glyphics upon one Sperm Whale in particular, I was much struck with a plate repre-
senting the old Indian characters chiselled
on the famous hieroglyphic palisades on the
banks of the Upper Mississippi. Like those
mystic rocks, too, the mystic-marked whale
remains undecipherable."*

These shapes and forms finally resolved into a set of mammary rudi-
ments—a mere suggestion of nipples, appearing in lines from the crotch
to the true breasts, to the armpits. They remained for some time, and
then disappeared.

Later, during the summer—with the intense heat beating up from
river, brick and asphalt, as it can only in St. Louis—he reported what
appeared to be Elephantiasis of the Scrotum—the scrotum swollen
and hanging to his knees, the penis enveloped, with only an invagina-
tion to indicate its presence. Whether he treated this condition, or
allowed it to pursue its course, in any case, he eventually recovered.

Over a considerable period of time, he lost several teeth. Nothing
seemed to happen to them, they didn't decay or cause pain—they
simply fell out. And, in every empty socket—after an extended delay
—he grew a replacement; so that, by the time the process ended, he
had, to a large extent, a third set of teeth.

At one time, he developed an abdominal swelling, so marked and painful it could not be ignored. For this, he went to the hospital, and
underwent surgery. The result was the removal of a teratoma, or
dermoid cyst—containing bits of skin, hair, nails, teeth and tongue,
fully developed. The only explanation was the predatory conquest by
Carl, at some very early prenatal stage, of an unfortunate, competitive
twin. The lesser organism, attacked and overcome, had nevertheless
managed to place random cells within the folds and envelopes of the

conquering embryo; and these, now fully developed, had waited until Carl's full growth to present themselves.

Recovering from the operation, he became involved in a drunken brawl. The trouble started in a tavern, spread to the sidewalk, and eventually to the whole block, and Carl, resisting the police, turned on an officer and attacked him. I never discovered the nature of the attack, but it put the officer in the hospital and Carl in jail.

Locked in solitary, in a cell remote from the others, Carl remained out of control, raving and screaming long after he was sober.

Then he suddenly became quiet. He began chatting with the guards, and, through them, sent messages to the other officers. In a short time, he was in a front office, having an interview . . . and a little after that, he was on the street, a free man, all charges dropped. He had simply conned his way out . . .

Once when I asked him about this, he laughed, put his arm on my shoulder, and quoted Melville, with appropriate flourish: ". . . men are jailors all; jailors of themselves."

. . . and added, matter-of-factly: "I liberated myself . . ."

For a while, Carl seemed to desert Concha, or at least two-time her. He took up with his final companion, a creature named Bonnie—fat, blowsy, alcoholic . . . she would sit in a rumpled bed, drunk, dirty, her stringy hair falling down, and quote Wordsworth and Keats . . . sneezing and weeping violently, lamenting that she suffered from "Rose Fever": unconsoled when Carl told her that Hart Crane, American poet, was similarly allergic . . .

Carl once bragged to me, confidentially, that he had accomplished intercourse with Bonnie twelve times during thirty hours . . .

Whatever else he did was mysterious . . . but the law was on his heels again—his position in St. Louis became untenable. Expecting to hear of his arrest, I was surprised to hear, instead, that he had committed himself to a private institution. It was a shrewd gesture: the police gradually lost interest in him, and yet, the commitment having been his own act, he was free to leave whenever the heat was off.

I tried very hard to locate him, but could find no trace—as usual, he had left no address. For many months, I knew nothing of him, and I began to feel that he was passing, or had already passed, into institutional oblivion.

F I V E

The New York Central train, westbound for St. Louis, rumbled out of the Indianapolis station, and I settled myself by the window, with little thought of sleep.

Slumping, I let my shoulder and the side of my head rest against the window. My bag was in the rack overhead, and in my pocket, my breast pocket, was the letter from Carl: I had, at long last, an address, and I was using it quickly, before it passed, like all the others, into obsolescence.

He had written of his discharge from the institution—and had taken the trouble to enclose a letter from the staff, proclaiming him cured. He announced, further, that he had opened a one-chair barbershop, in the old section of St. Louis, on 4th Street—and he went so far as to invite me to spend the week-end. Coming off the swing shift at midnight, I had packed my bag, and headed for the first train.

I thought of Carl as a barber, and wondered where and how he had learned this skill—or if he had taken the trouble to learn at all. My eyes closed, I became numbed, insulated, like the dim interior in which I was riding. I may have slept, I'm not sure; I had the sense, in any case, of entering and passing through something . . .

When I opened my eyes, there was gray in the sky. It was not dawn—just a dull, general lifting of the dark. We were in southern Illinois, the tracks slicing diagonally across flat, squared-off farm land. Snow remained on the ground, and occasional gusts of sleet and cold rain washed the outer glass.

I may have slept again. When I looked through the window, it was full day, though still overcast. But the land had changed, and I didn't quite understand how . . . the flatness was there, but there was a different tilt to it, a kind of flow, an imminence. Sitting up straight, I bought coffee and a dry cheese sandwich from a vendor. As the hot, strong liquid went down my throat, I realized that we were approaching St. Louis, and the river . . .

All at once, I understood why Carl had come here, to St. Louis, of all places; why California had been only a stopping place, and this, the Mound City, had become his inevitable destination. I could see ahead, in the distance, some elevations of earth: I couldn't tell whether these were part of the original Indian mounds, or railroad embankments, or perhaps part of the levee system. In any case, the contour was low, level and smooth; with the knowledge of the location of the city on the river, and the river's place in the face of the land, I realized that St. Louis was "home," the very eye and center of centripetal American geography, the land pouring in upon itself. I thought of China, and recalled that Carl's journey from there, from all that had happened there, was an eastward voyage, across half the globe; and, perhaps like Ishmael on board the Pequod, he was hunting back toward the beginnings of things; and, like the voyage of the Pequod,—or of any of the various caravels of Columbus that struck fierce weather returning from the Indies—perhaps Carl's eastward voyage, his voyage "home," was disastrous . . .

We entered East St. Louis, and the train slowed, as we passed through mile after mile of factory, tenement, dump and slum, an abandoned industrial desolation . . .

Rising over the earth mounds, the tracks entered a bridge, and we approached the river. The cold rainy wind blew waves onto the surface —dark black and purple, the wind squalls rushing across it, here and there turning a white cap. Through the steel girders I watched the water as long as I could see it. When we reached the other side, I felt that we had passed over a great hump . . .

Leaving the train at Union Station, I headed for 4th St., and had little trouble finding Carl. Tucked in a corner, in an ancient loft building, it looked like a poor spot for business. But the shop was open, and he was busy.

The sign read CARL AUSTIN MILLS, MASTER BARBER, and underneath, "I Need Your Head In My Business." As I opened the door, he looked up from his work, and I detected in his glance only surprise—I had not told him I was coming—and pleasure. Stepping forward, he offered me his hand, and his grip was familiar and sturdy—warmth and affection in it, such as he had seldom shown me, but nothing patronizing: it was the glad warmth of an animal. Returning to his customer, he gestured me to a chair, the sweep of his arm embracing and offering his hospitality, making rich and desirable the confines of his shop. He asked many friendly questions . . .

I looked around. Every inch of space, beyond what held his equipment, was taken up with pictures, decorations, objects of one sort or another. I had no idea how he had made such a collection. There were rocks, minerals, semi-precious stones of all shapes, sizes and colors, some of them shining. There were souvenirs and toys from every carnival and circus in the land. Airplane parts hung from the walls, a split half of a propeller was suspended on thin wires from the ceiling. Pictures, paintings and textile fragments appeared everywhere, the subjects ranging from Mayan, Aztec and Inca stone and art work, to movie stars, nude girls, and pornography. Relics from Alaska, and other Indian artifacts, were stuck on shelves. The magazine table included the morning newspaper, and thirty-year-old copies of the National Geographic and the Police Gazette. There was a settled look, a look of age . . .

Hanging in front of the mirror, directly back of the chair, so that strands of black hair descended among the bottles of oil and tonic, was the shrunken Indian head that he had won in a poker game in Alaska. Carl stepped back to survey his customer, his own great cranium coming close to the shrunken one . . .

He began telling a story—a wild tale about barbering among primitive Eskimos in Alaska, the natives being confused between haircuts and scalping. The customers seemed to know that he was lying, and this added to it . . .

I listened to him talk, watched him cut several heads of hair. The warmth of the shop entered me, became quieting. In addition to being a story-teller, he had a skill at his trade; his hands moved deftly over the men's heads, weaving a phrenological spell.

The city of St. Louis, with the advent of the railroads after the Civil War, had turned its back upon the river and faced westward, had abandoned the old continental blood stream . . . Carl, setting up in this section, hugging the river, now drew warehousemen, truckers, straggling barge- and riverboat-men from blocks, perhaps miles around . . .

I became sleepy, began to drowse in my chair. Carl gave me the key to his room, suggested that I take a nap . . . I was almost asleep, as I stumbled out the door.

He lived in a furnished room, not far from the shop. It was small, poor and bare, with the simplest furnishings—as barren of his personality as the shop was rich with it . . . too tired to look further, to dig beyond this front, I stretched across the bed and fell asleep.

When I awoke, it was mid-afternoon. Shaking myself, I sat on the edge of the bed, took a slower look around. On the floor, by the bed, were three books: a volume of Sappho, one of Homer, and the poems of Hart Crane . . .

Washing at the hand basin, I headed again for the shop. The rain had stopped, but cold wind blew off the river, pouring down the streets that led away from it.

A customer was just leaving and Carl was alone when I arrived. He suddenly decided to close, hustled me out and locked the door, before any one else showed up.

For several blocks we walked aimlessly, Carl—without coat or hat, his shirt open—sniffing the air like a dog. Then he stopped, clutched my elbow, and pointed . . . we turned and headed east, toward the river. A summer excursion boat was drawn up on the brick embankment, tilting at an angle. Together, just for the hell of it, we clambered aboard, laughing like kids, getting our feet soaked. I almost fell overboard when my foot slipped: Carl's hand flashed out, thrusting for my arm, and I got up safely.

Arms outstretched, balancing ourselves on the tilting planks, we made our way to the prow, and stood for some moments. The wind drove down on us from the north . . .

Melville:

> "*Natives of all sorts, and foreigners; men of business and men of pleasure; parlour men and backwoodsmen; farm-hunters and fame-hunters; heiress hunters, gold-hunters, buffalo-hunters, bee-hunters, happiness-hunters, truth-hunters, and still keener hunters after all these hunters. Fine ladies in slippers, and moccasined squaws; Northern speculators and Eastern philosophers; English, Irish, German, Scotch, Danes; Santa Fe traders in striped*

blankets, and Broadway bucks in cravats of cloth of gold; fine-looking Kentucky boatmen, and Japanese-looking Mississippi cotton planters; Quakers in full drab, and United States soldiers in full regimentals; slaves, black, mulatto, quadroon; modish young Spanish Creoles, and old-fashioned French Jews; Mormons and Papists; Dives and Lazarus; jesters and mourners, teetotallers and convivialists, deacons and blacklegs; hard-shelled Baptists and clay-eaters; grinning negroes, and Sioux chiefs solemn as high-priests. In short, a piebald parliament, an Anacharsis Cloots congress of all kinds of that multiform pilgrim species, man.

"As pine, beech, birch, ash, hackmatack, hemlock, spruce, basswood, maple, interweave their foliage in the natural wood, so these varieties of mortals blended their varieties of visage and garb. A Tartar-like picturesqueness; a sort of pagan abandonment and assurance. Here reigned the dashing and all-fusing spirit of the West, whose type is the Mississippi itself, which, uniting the streams of the most distant and opposite zones, pours them along, helter-skelter, in one cosmopolitan and confident tide."

Carl faced north, his whitened knuckles gripping the rail. I turned away, headed toward the vacant cabin, the river flowing south. In a moment he followed me, put his arm on my shoulder, and I felt again an animal affection. Huddled in my overcoat, tilted against the angle of the deck, I stood by him . . .

All at once, his body drew in upon itself; he gathered his jacket to his throat, clutched it with his free hand . . . he was chilled and threadbare, and the scrubby look of poverty came over him . . .

Melville:

"In the forward part of the boat, not the least attractive object, for a time, was a grotesque negro cripple, in towcloth attire and an old coal-sifter of a tambourine in his hand, who, owing to something wrong about his legs, was, in effect, cut down to the stature of a Newfoundland dog; his knotted black fleece and good-natured, honest black face rubbing against the upper part of people's thighs as he made shift to shuffle about, making music, such as it was, and raising a smile even from the gravest. It was curious to see him, out of his very deformity, indigence, and houselessness, so cheerily endured, raising mirth in some of that crowd, whose own

purses, hearths, hearts, all their possessions, sound limbs included, could not make gay.

"'What is your name, old boy?' said a purple-faced drover, putting his large purple hand on the cripple's bushy wool, as if it were the curled forehead of a black steer.

"'Der Black Guinea dey calls me, sar.'

"'And who is your master, Guinea?'

"'Oh, sar, I am der dog widout massa.'

"'A free dog, eh? Well, on your account, I'm sorry for that, Guinea. Dogs without masters fare hard.'

"'So dey do, sar; so dey do. But you see, sar, dese here legs? What ge'mman want to own dese here legs?'

"'But where do you live?'

"'All 'long shore, sar; dough now I'se going to see brodder at der landing; but chiefly I libs in der city.'

"'St. Louis, ah? Where do you sleep there of nights?'

"'On der floor of der good baker's oven, sar.'

"'In an oven? whose, pray? What baker, I should like to know, bakes such black bread in his oven, alongside of his nice white rolls, too. Who is that too charitable baker, pray?'

"'Dar he be,' with a broad grin lifting his tambourine high over his head.

"'The sun is the baker, eh?'

"'Yes, sar, in der city dat good baker warms der stones for dis ole darkie when he sleeps out on der pabements o' nights.'

"'But that must be in the summer only, old boy. How about winter, when the cold Cossacks come clattering and jingling? How about winter, old boy?'

"'Den dis poor old darkie shakes werry bad, I tell you, sar. Oh, sar, oh! don't speak ob der winter,' he added, with a reminiscent shiver, shuffling off into the thickest of the crowd, like a half-frozen black sheep nudging itself a cosy berth in the heart of the white flock."

Moving to the down-tilted side where we had climbed aboard, Carl and I clambered ashore, soaking our feet again. At the top of the embankment we turned, shivering in the wind, and looked back at the boat . . .

. . . it seemed shrunken, a toy, helpless on its perch of bricks.

We headed back into the city, chattering, half-running with cold. Carl made straight for a neon sign, with the word BAR . . .

We had some drinks, and wandered on . . . I tried to talk with him, or get him to talk, but his eyes looked beyond me, his mind held to no thought . . . he took one drink at a bar, and was off again.

Then again he turned to me, all warmth and consideration, his hand on my shoulder, the gesture affectionate, and firm . . .

As we wandered, the buildings became poorer, dirtier, more populous. Strange figures huddled in hallways, clustered around the doors of taverns—their lips thinned, thirsty, bitten back with poverty.

. . . at some time in the evening, we stood at the stage door of the burlesque theatre, while Carl tried to talk his way in . . . there was a glimpse of a near-naked girl . . .

Later, Carl ran out of money. I tried to loan him or give him some, offered him my wallet, everything I had—but he protested fiercely, the evening was to be his. The penurious, pinched look came over him . . . he reached into his pocket, took out a couple of linty crackers, and shared them with me . . .

> (and on the 4th voyage of Columbus the supply of biscuits became infested with worms . . . the men, refusing to remove these animals for fear of reducing the volume of food, took to eating only at night so they wouldn't have to see them . . .

We passed another bar, and Carl brought me to a halt. He stood for a moment . . . then cautioned me to wait outside, while he went in.

I watched him approach the first customer, standing at the rear end of the bar. They shook hands, Carl slapped his back, put a foot on the rail. The man gradually warmed, his body shifting, his coat hanging looser . . . they had a drink together, and the customer turned his back suspiciously to the rest of the room, drew something from his pocket, and he and Carl talked. After some moments, Carl drew back, placed his hand familiarly on the other's shoulder, his great head nodding assurances . . . and turned and came out the door. He said nothing . . . but at the next bar, he paid for drinks with a new $50 bill . . .

I have an image of the two of us—Carl stocky, broad-chested, jacket and shirt open to the rain, and I, slight, limping, hat and overcoat hanging sloppily on my frame—the two of us ambling side by side, drunk and speechless, a clown pair . . .

("Good friars and friends, behold me here /
A poor one-legged pioneer . . ."

The Melville line came to me as I pushed back the heavy door of a tenderloin tavern, the room cluttered with derelicts, sleeping, drinking, haranguing one another . . .

". . . a limping, gimlet-eyed, sour-faced person—it may be some discharged custom-house officer, who, suddenly stripped of convenient means of support, had concluded to be avenged on government and humanity by making himself miserable for life . . ."

". . . a lean old man, whose flesh seemed salted codfish, dry as combustibles; head, like one whittled by an idiot out of a knot; flat, bony mouth, nipped between buzzard nose and chin; expression, flitting between hunks and imbecile . . ."

". . . a singular character in a grimy old regimental coat, a countenance at once grim and wizened, interwoven paralysed legs, stiff as icicles, suspended between rude crutches, while the whole rigid body, like a ship's long barometer on gimbals, swung to and fro . . ."

Soaking, drinking in the words of The Confidence-Man, I leaned heavily across the bar, and turned to Carl. He seemed attentive, and I tried once more to get him to talk—asked him about the war, the POW camp, about Rico, Concha and California . . . for a moment, he was serious and sad . . .

Then he pounded me on the back, waved his arm, and presented to me one of the characters, crippled and bearded, who had come to beg a drink . . .

Carl ordered for him, swerved himself to the old man's misery:—a relation of hollow vowels, toothless and full of beer . . .

"After three years, I grew sick of lying in a grated iron bed alongside of groaning thieves and mouldering burglars. They gave me five silver dollars, and these crutches, and I hobbled off. I had an only brother who went to Indiana, years ago. I begged about, to make up a sum to go to him; got to Indiana at last, and they directed me to his grave. It was on a great plain, in a log-church yard with a stump fence, the old gray roots sticking all ways like moose-antlers. The bier, set over the grave, it being the last dug, was of green hickory; bark on, and green twigs sprouting from it.

Some one had planted a bunch of violets on the mound, but it was a poor soil (always choose the poorest soil for graveyards), and they were all dried to tinder. I was going to sit and rest myself on the bier and think about my brother in heaven, but the bier broke down, the legs being only tacked. So, after driving some hogs out of the yard that were rooting there, I came away, and, not to make too long a story of it, here I am, drifting down stream . . ."
(*Melville*)

Other derelicts left their tables, sidled toward us, clustering, jostling gently . . . Carl's arm swept out, gathered them in . . . every glass in the house was filled . . .

We passed the ruins of a cheap hotel, gutted by fire. Dark figures, cold and wet, stood about, staring at the stalagmites of charred wood . . . Carl spoke to one of them—he had been the night clerk, was still hovering over his job; he told us about the fire, about the man who drank rubbing alcohol, canned heat, and the like, and had managed to get his clothes soaked with the stuff, and then lit a cigarette—the bedding caught fire, the clerk had heard and seen him, screaming from his room, folded in blue flame . . .

Melville:

" . . . to the silent horror of all, two threads of greenish fire, like a forked tongue, darted out between the lips; and in a moment the cadaverous face was crawled over by a swarm of worm-like flames.

" . . . covered all over with spires and sparkles of flame, that faintly crackled in the silence, the uncovered parts of the body burned before us, precisely like phosphorescent shark in a midnight sea.

"The eyes were open and fixed; the mouth was curled like a scroll, and every lean feature firm as in life; while the whole face, now wound in curls of soft blue flame, wore an aspect of grim defiance, and eternal death."

Past midnight, Carl's manner became secretive, mysterious. For the first time, he began to move as though he had a destination, and this assurance made him the more devious, so that he acted

like Columbus, 4th voyage, treating the Indians with suspicion, misleading even the Sovereigns as to his navigations and discoveries . . .

("The seamen no longer carried charts because the Admiral had taken them all . . ."

141

or like Melville's Benito Cereno, a man trapped . . .

We walked down alleys and across vacant lots, pausing with grandiose watchfulness at the corners . . . more than once we doubled back on ourselves . . . at the corner of a narrow street, among warehouses, we stopped, smoked a cigarette, appeared casual . . . then moved slowly down the street, turned into an alley, and knocked at a lighted door. A man—short, bald-headed—opened after a moment, recognized and admitted Carl, and stared hard at me. I was passed, on Carl's word, and we moved through a long corridor, down some stairs, and, opening another door, entered a large, low-ceilinged room, filled with men, mostly middle-aged and beyond. Packing cases were set up at one side, serving as a bar, and there was a rudimentary stage, a raised platform, with overhead lighting, at the far end of the room. Nearby, a man beat notes out of a decrepit piano. Tables and chairs were scattered about, facing the stage. A few whores circulated among the men. We took a table, and I waited, looked around, while Carl went to the bar for drinks. The place had a familiar aspect, and I recognized it, from movies and TV, as a duplicate of the old western music hall and saloon —bar along the side, tables and chairs in the middle, stage across the end of the room. The girls were in character.

Carl picked up a girl at the bar, brought her back with him, sat her between us. She was a gorgeous negress. The lights in the room flashed and went out, leaving only the stage lights. The men applauded, took their seats . . .

In a moment, a girl appeared on the stage. Tall, blonde, she wore a green evening dress, covered with tiny spangles, and her equipment included various accessories—gloves, scarves, fake fur, a jacket—to be handled, manipulated, shifted and disposed of. She came to the front of the stage, so the light fell directly on her head and shoulders, creating shadows under her curves; she was still, hands held before her, her eyes, not calculating, not innocent, taking in the room.

The piano began to thump . . . the girl tapped her foot, her knee shaking the vertical lines of the gown . . . finger by finger, she removed one glove . . .

I sat back, the liquor, the closeness of the room, the people, the negress at my side, filling me. Carl and I lit cigars. There was satisfaction in the show, in the girl's presence on the stage, and I realized that in the flat gray of movies and television I had built up a hunger for just this: whatever the medium, just the flesh, here, in the room . . .

> (I recall, now, that, here in Indianapolis, the one burlesque theatre has been closed, to be converted into a revival hall . . .

> (as, in England, the Puritans closed the Elizabethan theatres, before getting to that other menace, the naked American Indian . . .

One by one the girl's accessories were removed and tossed aside. She stood in the strapless gown, at the very front of the stage, the light slanting on her from behind. There was, in her erect figure, an illusion of beauty, dignity, judgement, wisdom—of all desirable and satisfying values . . .

She turned, ambled upstage, and her hand went to the zipper in the small of her back . . .

> (and I thought that this was as intimate, as naughty as A Peep At Polynesian Life, Melville's Typee . . .

Turning again, she held the now unsupported gown with her fingers, cupping her breasts, practising all manner of delay and ruse, before revealing herself . . .

Carl leaned in front of the negress to speak to me, and I tilted toward him, so that our heads met over her breasts . . . the liquor had gone to his voice, as well as to my head, and I couldn't make out all that he said, but his manner was professorial, instructive—something about the importance of revelation, as opposed to objective study—the loss, in a society with a scientific bias, of the art of discovery . . . the negress remained immobile, her eyes flashing, a smile rich on her face . . .

Little by little, the performer's gown came off, to the applause of the hard-breathing men . . . she stood, displayed herself, in a g-string . . . the applause grew harder,

and my body froze: a negro, full black, appeared on the stage, stripped to the waist—the girl went to him, stood before him, facing front, and in the white light, his large, magnificent hands moved over her . . .

143

The quality of breathing in the room, the girl's eyes, all changed . . . I couldn't look at the dark girl beside me . . .

> (*Daggoo*, in *Moby-Dick*: "*Who's afraid of black's afraid of me! I'm quarried out of it!*"
>
> (*and Melville, elsewhere:* ". . . *as though a white man were anything more dignified than a white-washed negro.*"

I turned to Carl, just to see him rise, move to the back of the room, and the door . . . following him, I reached the door after he was already gone . . . I paused, glanced once more at the stage . . .

the girl was naked . . . the negro dropped to his knees before her, clutched her buttocks with his hands, and drew her toward him . . .

I found Carl on the sidewalk, his feet shifting, almost dancing, his eyes wild . . . as soon as I came up, he took off, and I struggled to keep up with him, following his back as fast as I could, down deserted streets and alleys . . . I ran as I had not run in years, perhaps never before, the light and heavy beat of my stride echoing from the buildings, the cold air burning in my lungs . . .

When I woke up, it was early morning, and I was sprawled across Carl's bed, hat and overcoat still on, my head hanging between bed and wall. I sat up, discovered Carl sitting on the floor, his head propped against the wall. He was surrounded by books and comic books, smoking a cigar, and reading

S U P E R M A N
in startling
3-D,

holding to his face the 3-dimensional glasses that come with the book —a bit of green cellophane before the left eye, and red before the right . . . turning the pages, laughing. Beside him, open at various places, were the volumes of Sappho, Homer and Crane that I had seen before, a good many more comic books . . . and a copy of Melville's Clarel.

Seeing me awake, he lit another cigar, handed it to me. I smoked, held my head in my hands, tried to reconstruct the evening. Carl finished Superman, picked up Clarel, and all at once, the tobacco went to my stomach ... I made a rush to the hand basin, was violently ill ...

> *(Melville: "While for him who would fain revel in tobacco, but cannot, it is a thing at which philanthropists must weep, to see such an one, again and again, madly returning to the cigar, which, for his incompetent stomach, he cannot enjoy, while still, after each shameful repulse, the sweet dream of the impossible good goads him on to his fierce misery once more—poor eunuch!"*

Staggering to the bed, I was galled to see Carl unmoved, reading. Shifting himself, expanding his diaphragm, holding Clarel before him, he read aloud:

> *"And he, the quaffer of the brine,*
> *Puckered with that heart-wizening wine*
> *Of bitterness, among them sate*
> *Upon a camel's skull, late dragged*
> *From forth the wave, the eye-pits slagged*
> *With crusted salt."*

I made it to the basin just in time, hung over it a long time ... there was nothing in me. When I got back to the bed, Carl had changed: not considerate, or even interested, he was watchful ... then his eyes went back to Clarel, and he read:

> *"... Sequel may ensue,*
> *Indeed, whose germs one now may view:*
> *Myriads playing pygmy parts—*
> *Debased into equality:*
> *In glut of all material arts*
> *A civic barbarism may be:*
> *Man disennobled—brutalized*
> *By popular science—"*

... he was declaiming, posturing outlandishly ... and he threw down the book, picked up Superman again, with the little red and green glasses ...

Squeezing my head in my hands, I closed my eyes. When I looked up, all color had vanished. Carl, the furniture, the room appeared in shades of gray . . . I blinked several times, my eyelids serving as the shutter of a movie camera, then closed my eyes . . .

and behind the closed lids, I saw the room in color, but in disconnected, monocular images, one for each eye . . . in addition, there was a partition, a wall, reaching from the wall of the room to the vertical center of my face, separating the two images . . .

I opened my eyes again, and was at once dizzy: everything that I saw was inverted, upside down . . . rolling onto the bed, I buried my face in the pillow . . .

I slept through most of the day . . . when I got up again, it was late afternoon, and I was alone. Though weak and hungry, I was slept out . . . my body was quiet. I stood by the bed for some moments . . . emptiness and loneliness—the loneliness of public rooms, of personal things used and not loved—entered me. Books were put away, basin washed, ash trays clean . . . Carl had erased himself from the room . . .

I found him at the shop—busy, loquacious, crisp—with no sign of fatigue. But his manner to me had changed . . . the warmth, the cordiality were gone, not deliberately, but in spite of himself, against his own will . . . I sat for some minutes, listening, chatting with him, trying to find what was there when I had first arrived, the morning before . . . but it was gone, the episode finished.

When he was between customers, I got up, prepared to leave. He followed me to the sidewalk, and we stood for some time at the corner, looking at the curb, at the street, at the gray darkening sky. It was already early evening, another night beginning—the streetlights and neon signs flickered on. Once more I tried to reach him, if only in a direct look from his eyes . . . he held my glance for an instant, and then changed—his posture, his manner, the very structure of his face—

146

something kin to the look of poverty that I had seen before, but not quite the same ... his shoulders collapsed inward, his eyes were downcast, his face troubled, his head moved restlessly ...

I thought of the purpose of this visit, of my coming to St. Louis: that I was trying only to reach him, to open a channel ... of how I had failed, how he had swept me into his own condition, and I had permitted it, allowed myself to become a part of all that he was caught in ...

> (*Melville: "From being cast away with a brother, good God deliver me!"*)

I thought of Melville, separated from Hawthorne ... and of Columbus, at Valladolid, no longer able to reach the court ...

I thought of China, the POW camp, of California and Joey: ... I thought that what is more terrible, even, than all that Carl had done, was the original misery of his being, of his coming to be in a condition that made it possible ...

> *Melville: "So true it is, and so terrible, too, that up to a certain point the thought or sight of misery enlists our best affections; but, in certain special cases, beyond that point it does not. They err who would assert that invariably this is owing to the inherent selfishness of the human heart. It rather proceeds from a certain hopelessness of remedying excessive and organic ill."*

I remembered the letter Carl had sent me, from the institution, announcing his complete cure ...

> *"So far may even the best men err, in judging the conduct of one with the recesses of whose condition he is not acquainted"* ...
> *Melville*

I put a hand on his shoulder, took his hand into my other ... he looked up, raised a smile, a little warmth ... but it was not Carl ...

The wind swept around the east corner ... he looked cold ... I gave him a squeeze, he slapped me on the shoulder, his chest expanding once more, and we parted ...

Some days later, back in Indianapolis, I got a postcard from him,

"Dear Herman: The Gin got here!"

and I didn't understand the significance, until I read Melville's letters to Hawthorne—the passionate pouring-out, the reach of one man to another—written in the froth of finishing <u>Moby-Dick</u>:

> *"It is a rainy morning; so I am indoors, and all work suspended*
> *. . . Would the Gin were here!"*

S I X

> *"'For Delly Ulver: with the deep and true regard and sympathy of*
> *Pierre Glendinning.*
>
> *"'Thy sad story—partly known before—hath now more fully*
> *come to me, from one who sincerely feels for thee, and who hath*
> *imparted her own sincerity to me. Thou desirest to quit this neigh-*
> *borhood, and be somewhere at peace, and find some secluded employ*
> *fitted to thy sex and age. With this, I now willingly charge my-*
> *self, and insure it to thee, so far as my utmost ability can go.*
> *Therefore—if consolation be not wholly spurned by thy great*
> *grief, which too often happens, though it be but grief's great folly*
> *so to feel—therefore two true friends of thine do here beseech thee*
> *to take some little heart to thee, and behink thee, that all thy life is*
> *not yet lived; that Time hath surest healing in his continuous*
> *balm. Be patient yet a little while, till thy future lot be disposed*
> *for thee, through our best help; and so, know me and Isabel thy*
> *earnest friends and true-hearted lovers.'"*

Melville, as Pierre . . . no longer chasing sperm oil monsters in the Pacific, or writing the hard syllables of <u>Ahab</u>, <u>Flask</u>, <u>Stubb</u> and <u>Star</u>-<u>buck</u> . . . but softened, turned inward, willingly charges himself to a "ruined" servant girl: <u>Delly Ulver</u> . . .

> *Pierre:* "*. . . this indeed almost unmans me . . .*"

The Pequod sunk and gone, Melville—1851 and '52—writes <u>Pierre</u> . . .

> <u>Woman Suffrage And Politics</u>, Catt and Shuler: "No cause ever made such rapid strides as that of Woman's Rights from 1850 to 1860."

> The New York <u>Herald</u>, September 7, 1853: "The assemblage of rampant

women which convened at the Tabernacle yesterday was an interesting phase in the comic history of the Nineteenth Century . . . a gathering of unsexed women, unsexed in mind, all of them publicly propounding the doctrine that they should be allowed to step out of their appropriate sphere to the neglect of those duties which both human and divine law have assigned to them."

and earlier, Abigail Adams, March, 1776, to her husband, sitting with the Continental Congress: ". . . and, by the way, in the new code of laws which I suppose it will be necessary for you to make, I desire you would remember the ladies and be more favorable to them than your ancestors. Do not put such unlimited power into the hands of husbands. Remember all men would be tyrants if they could. If particular care and attention are not paid to the ladies, we are determined to foment a rebellion . . ."

There is more, and earlier, in Melville: young Herman, age 21, shipped on a whaler to the Pacific:

"Weary with the invariable earth, the restless sailor breaks from every enfolding arm, and puts to sea in height of tempest that blows off shore. But in long night-watches at the antipodes, how heavily that ocean gloom lies in vast bales upon the deck; thinking that that very moment in his deserted hamlet-home the household sun is high, and many a sun-eyed maiden meridian as the sun."

. . . and there were the islands . . .

> *"In mid Pacific, where life's thrill*
> *Is primal—Pagan . . ."*

. . . Typee, Fayaway . . .

". . . the fair breeze of naked nature now blew in their faces."

> *"'Tis Paradise. In such an hour*
> *Some pangs that rend might take release."*

Back in New England and New York, throughout the long years . . . "pale years of cloistral life" . . . with Lizzie, the memory of Fayaway remained, dug in . . .

Pierre: "For whoso once has known this sweet knowledge, and then fled it; in absence, to him the avenging dream will come."

Dug in, avenging . . . for Melville came to accept Fayaway as original sin . . .

> *(1850, checks and underscores in the Old Testament: ". . . art thou come unto me to call my sin to remembrance . . ."*

. . . to accept that he had "ruined" her . . . and thus, locked in the old Christian myth, in the burden of Adam, he must make it up to all womankind:

as Pierre, to Delly . . .

as Herman, to Lizzie.

> *Mardi:* "*And thinking the lady to his mind, being brave like himself . . . he meditated suicide—I would have said, wedlock—and the twain became one.*"

> *I And My Chimney:* "*By my wife's ingenious application of the principle that certain things belong of right to female jurisdiction, I find myself, through my easy compliance, insensibly stripped by degrees of one masculine prerogative after another.*"

> *Fragments From A Writing Desk (written when he was 19):* "*What! to be thwarted by a woman! Peradventure baffled by a girl! Confusion! It was too bad! To be outgeneraled, routed, defeated by a mere rib of the earth? It was not to be borne!*"

And there was Benito Cereno, the Spaniard, captive of his blacks . . . sick of mind and body, loyally sustained (or so it seemed) by Babo, drifting at the mercy of the winds . . .

Melville as Cereno, captive not this time of the Typees, the friendly cannibals, but of his whites:

Lizzie, the Shaws, the right and just world (or so it seemed) of the 19th Century . . .

Lizzie as Babo, loyally sustaining Benito through misery . . .

> (and there was the other ship, the Bachelor's Delight, where all was trim and shipshape . . .

Clarel:

> "*My kin—I blame them not at heart—*
> *Would have me act some routine part,*
> *Subserving family, and dreams*

150

Alien to me—illusive schemes.
This world clean fails me . . ."

and

> *" 'Serve God by cleaving to thy wife,*
> *Thy children. If come fatal strife—*
> *Which I forebode—nay!' and she flung*
> *Her arms about him there, and clung."*

The rhyming couplets—Melville's aging force thrashing through eight hundred pages, two volumes, of <u>Clarel</u>. No longer the powering prose of <u>Moby-Dick</u>, mounting pilingly upon itself, but couplets: chains, darbies . . .

> (the beloved irons that Columbus hugged to himself, swore to die with

> (and did, the iron transmuted into his flesh, as arithritic gout . . .

Melville: ". . . so that the gallows presented the truly warning spectacle of a man hanged by his friends."

<u>Israel Potter</u>: *"The other officer and Israel interlocked. The battle was in the midst of the chaos of blowing canvas. Caught in a rent of the sail, the officer slipped and fell near the sharp edge of the iron hatchway. As he fell, he caught Israel by the most terrible part in which mortality can be grappled. Insane with pain, Israel dashed his adversary's skull against the sharp iron. The officer's hold relaxed, but himself stiffened. Israel made for the helmsman, who as yet knew not the issue of the late tussle. He caught him around the loins, bedding his fingers like grisly claws into his flesh, and hugging him to his heart. The man's ghost, caught like a broken cork in a gurgling bottle neck, gasped with the embrace. Loosening him suddenly, Israel hurled him from him against the bulwarks."*

Melville: still able to tire a Hawthorne:

> *Una, to her aunt: "Mr. Melville was here a day or two, and Mamma overtired herself during his visit, and was quite unwell for a day or two afterwards."*

. . . and Lizzie:

reported by Sam Shaw: "Elizabeth's catarrh is somewhat relieved here but I am sorry to see how generally feeble she is, and prematurely old."

Melville: growing older—Lizzie outlived him by many years—no longer able to thrash . . .

From The Career Of Mocha Dick: *"From first to last 'Mocha Dick' had nineteen harpoons put into him. He stove fourteen boats and caused the death of over thirty men. He stove three whaling vessels so badly that they were nearly lost, and he attacked and sunk a French merchantman and an Australian trader. He was encountered in every ocean and on every known feeding ground. He was killed off the Brazilian banks in August, 1859, by a Swedish whaler, which gathered him in with scarcely any trouble, but it was always believed that poor old 'Mocha Dick' was dying of old age."*

There was Columbus, 4th voyage, forbidden by the Court to enter the principal island he had discovered . . .

"Moreover every man had it in his power to tell me that the new Governor would have the superintendence of the countries I might acquire."

. . . cruising elsewhere in the Caribbean, battling tempests and Indians, his ships rotting . . .

Ferdinand: "Being here at anchor ten leagues from Cuba, full of hunger and trouble, because they had nothing to eat but hard-tack and a little oil and vinegar, and exhausted by working three pumps day and night because the vessels were ready to sink from the multitude of worms that had bored into them . . ."

. . . putting ashore finally on Jamaica, where the two ships, the Capitana and Santiago, lashed together, beached, worm-eaten and rotten, ended their careers as houseboats . . .

. . . isolated among his islands—no tools for re-planking or building, his caulkers dead, his crew in mutiny, no ship likely to call as he had earlier reported no gold in Jamaica—Columbus survived for over a year on what food the Indians brought him, living on the arrested caravels . . .

There is the old Spanish proverb: "La verdad no se casa con nadie" . . .

and Melville: "Truth will not be comforted."

Shifting in my chair, I become aware again of the house, the attic, the rafters—poised in the quiet of the city, the dark, early-morning hours. I think of the early days in Indiana, the first settlements. I think of my great-grandfather, Hammond Mills, who built this house—and of his well-worn philosophy: The Mind is to the Body as the Whole Man is to the Earth . . .

I remember fragments of medical school, the boys and men I studied and lived with . . . one became a gynecologist and surgeon, now has a lucrative, busy practice here in the city, scraping out the female troubles of Indiana . . . another has a commission in the Navy, does brilliant research in Space Medicine: the problems raised by sending human beings into outer space . . .

Shifting again, I am invaded with bitterness: I think of us as a nation of prurient neuters, bald-headed oglers, the men having laid down original tools and taken up others: become science fictioneers, space shippers, nuclear mystics, relinquishing the Body (Earth), seeking to escape it, save only to peer at it naughtily . . . become, with the aid of popular religion, the modern devout of the ether . . .

There is the population—not only of our own country but of the world —become anaplastic, growing, since World War II, wildly, without roots or viable form . . .

the cells reverting to simplest, undifferentiated forms, breaking down so rapidly as to lose all trace of roots, of origin . . .

S E V E N

I lost track of Carl once again. Letters to both the shop and the room were returned by the post office.

When word came, after many weeks, it was not from Carl, but from doctors at the mental hospital, where he had again been committed. He had finally told them about me, had given them my address, and they wanted me to come: he was violent, and they thought I might help . . .

I boarded the train after midnight, as before. I was no longer interested in motion, in adventure . . . the journey was repetition, return over old ground . . . the fact of direction, of heading west, was not exciting: I was moving from one city to another, a simple act of travel, without meaning . . .

I thought of Carl, as my older brother—and I thought of Herman's older brother, Gansevoort, who failed in business, then in politics, and, heavily in debt, died, age 30, of "nervous derangement . . ."

> *Herman, writing to Gansevoort—unaware that the latter had already died: "Remember that composure of mind is every thing."*
>
> *and later, writing of another: "This going mad of a friend or acquaintance comes straight home to every man who feels his soul in him,—which but few men do. For in all of us lodges the same fuel to light the same fire. And he who has never felt, momentarily, what madness is has but a mouthful of brains."*

Tearing apart the paper cup from which I had finished my coffee, I scribbled a few lines on it:

In Memoriam: Gansevoort Melville

> **who fails in business**
> **goes to politics;**
> **who fails in politics**
> **goes to heaven.**
>
> **(who fails in all**
> **goes to whale . . .**

> *and I thought of the contemporary review of Moby-Dick: ". . . so much trash belonging to the worst school of Bedlam literature . . ."*

Arrived in St. Louis, I went straight to the hospital, and the doctor in charge of Carl admitted me to his office.

I asked about Carl. He said that he was periodically violent, and for this reason was kept in restraint. He was at present in isolation, in a straight jacket. I stood up, paced nervously across the floor—exploiting in my own body the motion denied to Carl. I suggested that whatever else was the matter with him, whatever therapy they might be planning for him, it should be oriented in his having the simplest of personal freedom—that what he needed, first and foremost, was space . . .

The doctor looked at me candidly for a moment, and then begged me to follow him—we went out of the office, down a corridor, by elevator to another floor, around several corners, and into a room where masons and carpenters were at work. Motioning the workers aside, he showed me where Carl had terrorized a group of inmates: with nothing but his bare hands, he had ripped the paneling from a window frame, removed the window, and, unable to bend the iron bars, had dug with his finger-ends into the stonework and masonry itself . . .

> (*Moby-Dick:* "*How can the prisoner reach outside except by thrusting through the wall?*"

I asked to see Carl, and the doctor readily assented. We passed through various other parts of the hospital, catching glimpses of patients, in private and public rooms, in varying states . . .

> *Melville: "I have been in mad-houses full of tragic mopers, and seen there the end of suspicion: the cynic, in the moody madness muttering in the corner; for years a barren fixture there; head lopped over, gnawing his own lip, vulture to himself; while, by fits and starts, from the corner opposite came the grimace of the idiot at him."*

We found Carl standing, spread-legged, defiant, in the middle of his barren room. The jacket made him appear armless. He began at once to speak, to declaim:

> **"But this notion, that science can play farmer to the flesh, making there what living soil it pleases . . ."**

> **"Try to rid my mind of it as I may, yet still these chemical practitioners with their tinctures, and fumes, and braziers, and occult incantations, seem to me like Pharaoh's vain sorcerers, trying to beat down the will of heaven."**

The words were familiar, though I wasn't sure of the source . . .

> **"Please," I said, turning to the doctor, "take off the jacket..."**

He hesitated a moment, and then complied.

Carl, standing rigid while the doctor untied the tapes, declaimed again:

> **"Begone! You are all alike. The name of doctor, the dream of helper, condemns you. For years I have been but a gallipot for your experimentisers to rinse your experiments into, and now, in this livid skin, partake of the nature of my contents.**

Begone! I hate ye."

He held his arms to his body for some time after they were free. Slowly then, he unlimbered, heaving his shoulders . . .

The doctor warned that he would be outside if he were needed—and he left us alone.

Carl turned to me—and I recalled what it was he was quoting: <u>The Confidence Man</u> . . .

> "A sick philosopher," he continued ominously, "is incurable."

His body shifted, the defiance went out of it, and a warmth came in, clumsy and affectionate. Raising an arm, he clasped my shoulder, drew me toward him.

> "Mike, boy," he said—this was the first indication that he recognized me—"Mike, boy, there's something I want to tell you . . ."

Bowing his head, he screwed his brow, punched it with thumb and forefinger. He looked up suddenly, declaimed again, vaguely, in fright rather than defiance:

> "He tried to think—to recollect,
> But the blur is on his brain."

I began to wonder when in his career he had read so much Melville—read him so well that he had memorized whole passages. Or perhaps he had never actually read him . . . maybe Melville, as history, had impressed himself into the fibre and cells of which Carl was made, had become part of his makeup . . .

He was sad now, unable to remember what he wanted to tell me, still clutching my shoulder.

> "The Indians . . ." he began—this time he was not quoting—and he breathed hard, letting the sentence hang for some moments . . .

> "The Indians shrank the heads of their enemies . . ."—again he breathed hard—". . . and we . . ."

> "we shrink the hearts of our friends." He gripped my shoulder, released it, and turned away . . .

Again, his mood changed, became matter-of-fact. He went to the bed, lifted the mattress, took out some papers—scribblings, drawings of one sort or another. We sat down together, and he passed them to me, one at a time.

There was a flower picture, rich and luxuriant, the paper covered all over with blossoms. Showing it to me, he waved his hand in free, abstract motions, to suggest the manner of drawing it. There was a title in the corner: "Herbage, not verbiage."

The next drawing was a vague impression, in good anatomy, of a woman's womb, drawn as a transparent membrane: inside it, occupying the entire space was the head of an aged man, with a straight, gray beard . . .

He shoved another paper into my lap, became suddenly angry. It was a tortured, twisted figure, nailed to a cross.

> thrusting his finger at the face, shouting: "There's the first sonofabitch! The first coward!" and then, sardonically: "the first bastard that couldn't control his imagination . . ."

He stood up, still angry, and stalked about the room, as I read another paper:

ST. LOUIS MOTEL
1953
CARL AND BONNIE

<u>Carl</u>:
    bonnie bonnie bonnie bonnie bonnie baw
    buh buh buh

                waga
                  waga

gwama   gwama
bay   bay   bay
    bwana   bwana-bwana
bay bay bay bay bay,   buh
          Wanna!
bwana.
          great gorny
          hag-worm,
              wagon horn,
Oooooowwwwwwwwwww!

Bonnie:

Bog the corg

Carl:

Anny wen hog,

Ug.

waaaaaaaaaa!   waaaaaaaaaaaaaaaaaaaaaaaaaaaaaaaaaaaaaaaaaaaa!

waaaaaaaaaaaaaaaa!

¡ʁʁʁʁʁʁʁʁʁʁʁʁʁʁʁʁʁʁʁʁʁʁʁʁʁʁʁʁʁʁʁʁʁʁʁM

Aw, the wa!

Daw, the long wa!

Wa!

hih!

Bonnie:

shinny boy,

long wog,

flabble

Carl:

l o n g   w o g !

flat.

agon worn,

apple!   apple!   apple!   apple!

schnad pool, blamble blan blag blzz

waw

W a a a a a a a a a a a a a w

Bonnie:

flamble   flamble

I looked up, found him angry, posed.

"Go mad I can not: I maintain
The perilous outpost of the sane."

and he laughed, roared, at the quote from Clarel—the book of chains.

158

(Lizzie, when Herman was writing it: "If ever this dreadful incubus of a book (I call it so because it has undermined all our happiness) gets off Herman's shoulders I do hope he may be in better mental health—but at present I have reason to feel the gravest concern & anxiety about it— to put it in mild phrase . . .")

and Herman, in a footnote to a letter: "N. B. I ain't crazy."

The doctor came in, with an attendant. Carl, as one of the violent, was scheduled for hydrotherapy, which consisted of stripping the patients, herding them together at the end of a tiled room, and playing streams of water on them, at firehose pressure, in an effort to quiet them.

I protested that Carl was already quiet, that there was no need for it, but it made no difference—his name was on the list. He was cowed, his shoulders caving, as they led him away.

A news item from Honolulu—1854:

> "*Our readers will doubtless recollect the narrative published in the year 1851, respecting the whale ship 'Ann Alexander,' Capt. Dublois, being stove by a sperm whale in the Pacific ocean. Recently Capt. D. visited Honolulu . . . We learned from him many striking and remarkable circumstances respecting the attack . . . Without repeating the story we would state, that about five months subsequently, the same whale was taken by the 'Rebecca Sims,' Capt. Jernegan. Two harpoons were discovered in the whale, marked 'Ann Alexander.' The whale's head was found seriously injured, and contained pieces of the ship's timbers. He had lost his wildness and ferocity, being very much diseased . . .*"

Later, walking down the corridor, I heard the hollering and shrieking of the inmates as the hoses were turned on them—and I recognized, above the others, the vast, bellowing tones of Carl, urging out of his lungs, in defiance of the water streams, hollow vowels . . .

EIGHT

There was talk, in Carl's case, of performing a frontal lobotomy—cutting into the frontothalamic fibres (the white matter) of the frontal lobes of the brain . . . but, in correspondence with the doctors, I was able to discourage it . . .

Instead, he was given different forms of convulsion therapy—electro-shock when either violent or calm, and metrazol, when in deep melancholy . . .

I thought of Moby-Dick, and Pierre . . . of a man sinking, pulling down and over him his family, his parents and ancestors—the mutations of all evolution—

struggling convulsively, even in drowning, to re-form himself, to grow or discover a new center . . .

as an epileptic, or in syncope: to fight out of the wrong center and into the right,

or to the left of it . . .

and I thought of the doctors, with electronics and drugs—one remove from his own, self-determined spasms of epilepsy—trying to force Carl

to create a new source and origin of motion . . .

NINE

Right after the First World War, when Carl and I were both small children, my father, encouraged by the Federal Farm Loan Act of 1916, added heavily to his holdings, paying exorbitant figures, assuming large mortgages, for adjacent farm land. We already had more than we could manage . . . but he wouldn't be stopped. In 1921, the bubble burst . . . our land dropped in value to less than half what we had paid for it, what we were committed to in mortgages. The prosperous Twenties, enjoyed by the rest of the nation, never existed for the farmer . . .

We were forced to sell—or, we thought at the time that we had sold. Father, in a state of despair and confusion, turned the affairs over to Mother, and she somehow managed, without telling the rest of us, to hang onto the house and enough of the land to be rented (the income to be applied against mortgages and debts) . . .

> (clinging to the land, as Columbus struggled, and failed, to hold the Indes . . .

. . . so that today, after the years of poverty, I and my family may enjoy once again the old house—a rural island, all but swallowed into the city . . .

We left Indianapolis, moved to Terre Haute—"high ground"—center of the Indiana coal mines,

birthplace of Theodore Dreiser, and Eugene V. Debs . . .

Down payment was put on a mean, one-story house, in a crowded part of the city. Failing to scrape a living out of the earth as a farmer, Father wanted to dig under the surface: he took a job in the mines . . .

Work was part-time at first . . . we skimped, saved and mended. In 1922, just when he went on full shift and the job became steady, the miners were called out on strike: Father was idle for nine bitter months . . .

Theodore Dreiser: born, Terre Haute, 1871, twenty years before Melville died, and a thousand miles deeper in the land . . . so that he was full grown by the time Melville put down his pen . . .

The house on Ninth Street in Terre Haute, where Paul and Sarah Dreiser lived, was infested with spirits and night-striders. On the night of Theodore's birth, "Three maidens, brightly garbed, with flowers in their hair, danced into Sarah's room and out again, to disappear seemingly into the air; and when afterward the boy himself proved perilously puny and sickly, inimical forces seemed to be in command."

The family was poor . . . Theodore was sent home from school one winter, because it was too cold to be without shoes. He was ashamed to be seen carrying the laundry his mother took in, or stealing coal, lump by lump, from between the railroad tracks. When an old watchman died—a man he had known and who had been kind to him—he went to stare at the remains, saw the two coins on the eyelids, and reached for them . . .

and there was the father, Paul Dreiser: a transient, a failure, moving

161

from house to house, one jump ahead of the mortgage . . .

I recall my own father: he had become interested in Socialism, talked about the life and work of Eugene Debs:

born, Terre Haute, 1855, when the ripples had scarcely ceased lapping, or the water become smooth, over the sinking of the Pequod . . . organized first industrial union (1893), led the Pullman strike ('94) . . . helped organize, 1900, the Socialist Party, polled nearly a million votes for President (1920), campaigning from prison against Harding, and, at the time of the coal strike—1922—was still living . . .

I recall Father, during the strike, sitting at the kitchen table (in different kitchens, of different houses, each meaner than the one before), his face bland, naive, confident—no longer the man who had worked twelve, fourteen hours a day on the farm, who, with his own main strength, had held the house together during a tornado—replying, now, to most any question with a remark about Debs: he had faith in Gene, old Gene would help us, would take care of us . . . while Mother got a meal for a family of four out of a loaf of stale bread (sold, for a few pennies, at the back door of the bakery), and a jar of the precious, guarded, hoarded tomatoes—treasured above all other possessions— that she had put up years back, on the farm . . .

young Dreiser, taking refuge from his troubles, would get up early in the morning, walk into the country with his dog, to study the spider webs and morning glories, the wrens and swallows . . .

> (as, in the Gulf of Paria, Columbus observed the tiny oysters clinging to the mangrove roots: the oyster shells open, to catch from the leaves above, dewdrops that engender pearls . . .

The strike finally over, Father went back to work, his confidence in some measure restored. Mother had somehow managed to hold the family together . . .

and Dreiser, his mother dead, his father become impossible to live with, moved—1891, the year of Melville's death—to Chicago, to the slums: the smell of sour beer, sewer gas and uric acid . . .

took to writing, produced a novel: Sister Carrie, written during the years 1899 and 1900, and standing therefore at the entrance, the beginning of the 20th Century . . .

Theodore Dreiser: gate-keeper, janitor to the century, presiding over the entrance upon and beginning of things,

>   (and Debs, 1900, formed the Socialist
>   Party...

Dreiser had his troubles getting the thing published: signed a contract with a publisher—but the publisher's wife objected strenuously (Carrie was not moral), and they pulled a fast one: published, according to contract (minimum edition)—and stored the books in the basement...

Pierre, dealing with incest, was produced without question—but that was earlier, the pioneer days... by now—1900—Progress had become Serious Business: adulterous Carrie was stuffed in the cellar...

and in both books we have the spectacle of a man sacrificing and ruining himself... Pierre and Isabel, in the classic tragedy, end as suicides, whereas, in Dreiser's work, Hurstwood vanishes a derelict, and Carrie is left idle, floating into the new century:

> *"In your rocking-chair, by your window, shall you dream such
> happiness as you may never feel."*

As the failure of Moby-Dick and Pierre broke Melville's health, so Carrie's failure broke Dreiser's. Living in New York, bankrupt, alone, he suffered hallucinations, his eyes itched and stung, his left eye became weaker, lost its power of accommodation... sitting or standing, he found himself compelled to turn around, to go in a circle, to bring himself into alignment with something... he nearly jumped into the East River...

>   (when he had first come to New York, first
>   approached the ocean, he felt small and
>   trivial...

>   (the vast ocean, into which Hart Crane
>   leaped...

>   (where Melville had been so much at home
>   ...

*Sister Carrie: "She also marvelled at the whistles of the hundreds
of vessels in the harbor—the long, low cries of the Sound steamers
and ferryboats when fog was on. The mere fact that these things
spoke from the sea made them wonderful. She looked much at*

*what she could see of the Hudson from her west windows and of
the great city building up rapidly on either hand. It was much to
ponder over . . ."*

From Terre Haute, Father and Mother, Carl and I moved to Sullivan,
where the job in the mines was steady, and the pay better . . .

(this being another of the towns where
Dreiser had lived, as a child . . .

and my hand reaches across the desk for the clipping, yellowed with
age, from the 1925 newspaper: mother saved and passed it on to me,
and I cannot bring myself to dispose of it:

FIFTY-ONE ARE
KILLED IN BIG
MINE EXPLOSION

**Greatest Disaster in His-
tory of Indiana
Coal Fields.**

**ALL TRAPPED ARE
BELIEVED KILLED**

**More Than Hundred Men
in Mine at the Time
of Blast.**

(BY THE ASSOCIATED PRESS)

SULLIVAN, Ind., Feb. 20—Fifty-one men are believed to have been killed
almost instantly today in an explosion of gas in the City Coal Company mine on
the outskirts of the city, that wrought the greatest mine disaster in the history of
the Indiana Coal Fields.

There were 121 miners in the mine at the time of the explosion which occurred
in the third and fourth entries North where most of the men killed were at work.

*(Melville, in the cave of Sybil: "What in
God's name were such places made for, &
why? Surely man is a strange animal. Diving into the bowels of the earth rather than
building up towards the sky. How clear an
indication that he sought darkness . . ."*

The work of bringing out the dead proceeded slowly, the bodies being brought
singly. Rescue workers were handicapped by gas fumes which flooded the mine
immediately after the explosion.

164

I recall standing beside Mother—Carl on the other side, a hand of hers reaching to each of us—waiting, hour after hour, not moving ... and when the body was brought up, the faces of the others turned toward us—curiosity locked in compassion—Mother waiting (Carl and I looking to her, even though it be disaster, wanting to be sure), waiting until the body were brought before her—and, as she recognized him, Father, her hand clutching, tightening ...

Most authentic reports of the accident were that the explosion occurred when miners either cut into abandoned workings or a slight cave-in opened old entries in which gas had collected, the miners' lamps setting off the pocket of gas ...

Men who had been in the mine said the explosion seemed to go in gusts, some being suffocated, others horribly burned, while others were but slightly burned. Many were hurled about rooms and entries ...

Rope lines established by local authorities and miners failed to check the rush of hundreds who flocked to the mine.

(...rushing, eddying to the disaster...

there was the long period of waiting, and discovery—the knowledge, in the pit of my stomach, that something had happened, the excitement, the image of his face, as Carl and Mother and I saw it before us, his body—waiting for the realization, the understanding of it to burst upon me ...

like a holiday: the normal, daily laws of living abrogated—waiting to discover what it was, what it meant, that Father was dead ...

...followed by disappointment, as there was no discovery, no bursting upon me, but only dullness, a slow seepage of understanding ... and the poverty doubled in, feeding upon itself, as we lived now, a family of three, on the compensation—$13.20 a week—allowed by the law ...

with the numbness: the absence of Father, who, even in failure, had provided a dimension that was now gone ...

Where Melville dove, Dreiser floated ... a great mass of pity, cut off ...

Hurstwood, in Sister Carrie, as Dreiser's father, sitting alone, apathetic in his rocker:

"Hurstwood saw her depart with some faint feelings of shame,

*which were the expression of a manhood rapidly becoming stulti-
fied.*"

and the drear, the cold, wint'ry drear of Hurstwood, struggling to re-
claim himself as a $2-a-day scab in the Brooklyn trolley strike . . .

Dreiser, who was sterile—terminating his sons before their conception, giving them, therefore, shorter lives, shorter agonies than Melville's sons—nevertheless took the trouble, on a trip to Europe, to
hunt out his father's birthplace . . .

searching the sources, the roots, the blasted paternity . . .

Theodore Dreiser, Indiana-born, doorkeeper of the century . . .

> (in ancient Rome, the double barbican gate
> in the Forum—dedicated to Janus, su-
> preme janitor—was closed during times of
> peace, open only in war . . .

B U D

O N E

AFTER Moby-Dick, the sinking, Melville, with pseudonyms and anonyms, kept trying to die, as Pierre . . .

> "*. . . death-milk for thee and me!*"

Benito Cereno . . .

> "*seguid vuestro jefe*"

and Bartleby the Scrivener . . .

> *opening lines, written when he was 34: "I am a rather elderly man."*

and like Columbus, in search of death, he turned to the Holy Land, Sodom, the Dead Sea . . .

> "*. . . foam on beach & pebbles like slaver of mad dog—smarting bitter of the water,—carried the bitter in my mouth all day— bitterness of life—thought of all bitter things—Bitter is it to be poor & Bitter, to be reviled, & Oh bitter are these waters of Death, thought I.—Old boughs tossed up by water—relics of pick-nick— nought to eat but bitumen & ashes with dessert of Sodom apples washed down with water of Dead Sea.— . . .*"

and Columbus, following the 3rd voyage, liberated from his chains by the Sovereigns,

> (as Melville had been liberated, temporarily, from the chains of poverty, by

Judge Shaw,

turned inland

(as Melville turned inland, in Pierre,

to another scheme: the liberation of Jerusalem ...

retiring to the convent of Las Cuevas, he began work on the Book of
Prophecies:

> "St. Augustine says that the end of this world is to come in
> the seventh millenary of years from its creation ... there are
> only lacking 155 years to complete the 7000, in which year the
> world must end."

> "The greatest part of the prophecies and Sacred Writing is
> already finished."

thus foreclosing on the future of the hemisphere he had discovered,

... condoning and justifying all brutalities against the Indians, as extreme haste must be made to convert the heathen ...

Melville:

> *"With wrecks in a garret I'm stranded ..."*

and

> *"Pleased, not appeased, by myriad wrecks in me."*

Columbus, on Jamaica:

> "Solitary in my trouble, sick, and in daily expectation of
> death ..."

and back in Spain, 1504, still trying to get to the Court to present his
claims and grievances—too weak and ill to make the trip on foot or on
horseback—requests the loan of a funeral bier from the Cathedral of
Seville:

> "This day, their Worships ordered that there should be
> loaned to the Admiral Columbus the mortuary bier in which
> was carried the body of the Lord Cardinal Don Diego Hurtado
> de Mendoza, whom may God have in his keeping, in order
> that he may go to the Court, and a guarantee was taken from
> Francisco Pinelo which assured the return of the said bier to
> this church in safety."

... to be carried out of his disaster like Ishmael, on the floating coffin ...

T W O

But Melville, after trying through the long middle years to die, put out
a late, late bloom ...

> *(scores & underscores, in a volume of Thomas*
> *Hood: ". . . the full extent of that poetical*
> *vigour which seemed to advance just in pro-*
> *portion as his physical health declined."*

... in his sixties and seventies, came to life:

> *"We the Lilies whose palor is passion ..."*

> *". . . the winged blaze that sweeps my soul*
> *Like prairie fires ..."*

> *"To flout pale years of cloistral life*
> *And flush me in this sensuous strife."*

> *"The innocent bare-foot! young, so young!"*

> *"The plain lone bramble thrills with Spring"*

> *"The patient root, the vernal sense*
> *Surviving hard experience ..."*

In a volume, transparently dedicated to Lizzie:

> *". . . white nun, that seemly dress*
> *Of purity pale passionless,*
> *A May-snow is; for fleeting term,*
> *Custodian of love's slumbering germ ..."*

> *"I came unto my roses late.*
> *What then? these gray hairs but disguise,*
> *Since down in heart youth never dies ..."*

> *"Time, Amigo, does but masque us—*
> *Boys in gray wigs, young ..."*

and elsewhere:

> *"Could I remake me! or set free*
> *This sexless bound in sex, then plunge*
> *Deeper than Sappho, in a lunge*
> *Piercing Pan's paramount mystery!*
> *For, Nature, in no shallow surge*
> *Against thee either sex may urge . . .*

Sappho, and Hart Crane . . .

surely, if Melville died before he was born, then, too, he was born before he died . . .

. . . and on the 4th voyage, aging and ill, forbidden by the Sovereigns to enter San Domingo, Columbus set sail for that very port. Ovando, the new governor, busy with a fleet of 28 vessels embarking for Spain, refused to admit the Admiral . . . on board the fleet were Francisco Bobadilla, who earlier had chained Columbus; Francisco Roldan, arch-rebel; and a rich cargo of West Indian gold . . .

Columbus warned them not to sail, that a storm was brewing . . .

perhaps he noted an oily swell from the southeast, abnormal tides, oppressive air, veiled cirrus clouds, gusty winds on the water's surface, brilliant sunset illuminating the sky, and large numbers of seal and dolphin on the surface . . .

(as well as twinges in rheumatic joints . . .

But the others laughed, called him a diviner and a prophet,

(Like Melville, in Clarel, predicting for the New World:

> ("*Not only men, the state lives fast—*
> *Fast breeds the pregnant eggs and shells,*
> *The slumberous combustibles*
> *Sure to explode . . .*"

Ovando's fleet set out boldly, under full sail: headed into the full blast of the storm . . .

Later, when all but 3 or 4 of the 28 ships had gone down, with all hands lost—his enemies accused the old discoverer of having raised the tempest himself, by magic art . . .

THREE

When I went to St. Louis a third time, Carl was out of the hospital. It was pleasant weather—brisk and sunny—and he met me at the station with a borrowed car—a '51 Plymouth station wagon.

There was vigor in his face, freshness in his actions. He had a crew haircut, and was sunburned. Standing at the train gate, his collar turned up, legs spread apart, hands thrust in his pockets, he looked boyish and strong.

> (It wasn't until after I had left him, when I was on my way back to Indianapolis, that I realized he had said nothing about what he was doing, where he was living, what his plans were—so completely was he taken up with the present moment—so thoroughly did he capture my assurances . . .

We headed west on U.S. 40, out of the city. I recalled Carl's driving from childhood—from the first time he massacred the corn field on a tractor. No less erratic now, he talked volubly, gestured with one hand and the other, moved his feet restlessly over the pedals—glanced only occasionally at the road, appropriating it as he wished.

He told me that U.S. 40 follows old animal and Indian trails, westward migration trails. It was known for a time as the Boone's Lick Trail, for the salt lick developed by Daniel Boone and his sons. Carl told me— bouncing his broad rump, spreading his arms as he talked—how Boone had moved out here because he wanted more elbow room, Kentucky had become too crowded . . .

> (Melville: "You must have plenty of sea-room to tell the Truth in . . ."

There was the stage driver in 1840, Carl mentioned, who, when the road became too muddy and full of ruts, drove out on the prairie, made a new road . . .

Reaching St. Charles, we turned off the highway, headed southwest over back roads, along the Missouri River. We came into rich farming country, with fine old brick houses: long, sloping shingled roofs, and generous porches. Carl mellowed as we rambled, became less talkative, and warmer, his chest expanding with the rolling orchards and fields of corn, timothy, alfalfa and oats.

The midday sun warmed us, and we got out of the car, walked down a deep creek valley to the river's edge. Carl had brought along some cooked pork chops and a loaf of honest German bread . . . I had a bottle of redeye that I'd brought from home . . . we sat on the grass, near a patch of willows, and ate and drank, soaked in the sun that would be warm only through the broad noon hours . . .

We talked of Indiana, of Mother and Father, of the old days, and of ourselves. With yankee and rebel blood in us—joining and hanging on in the prairie—we wanted to know the difference between north and south . . . we recalled that whenever Mother thought about something, she "allowed" it was so, whereas Father "kalklated" it . . . we thought of rivers and small streams—"brooks" in the North and "branches" in the South—and of the pioneer landing on the southern coast, following the main streams inland, or perhaps turning off on a branch, while the northern pioneer found the rivers—the Merrimac, the Connecticut, the Hudson, the Delaware—coming out of the North and therefore heading in no useful direction: to be crossed, rather than followed . . .

. . . the rivers therefore becoming allies to the southerners, and, to the yankees, obstacles, to be out-smarted and overwhelmed—as the North eventually out-smarted and overwhelmed the South. To the one, nature was objective, to be studied: the bird and flower books were written in the north, and Carl recalled the president of Indiana University, back in the last century, who must have been a yankee: claiming that prayer could be used to arrest the laws of nature . . . the other, the southerner, was in and of nature, immersed in her . . . the likes of Daniel Boone . . .

Going barefoot, rolling up his trousers, Carl stepped into the chill, muddy water. The river, charged with fresh rains, was swift and treacherous . . . he held his hand out to me, and I stripped off shoes and socks, followed him in. Steadying each other, we walked out to our knees . . . we could see around a bend upstream, where the water was eating out the bank, undermining some poplars . . . now and then a stump or a full tree swept past us . . . leaning toward me, clutching my hand, shouting above the rush of the waters, Carl asked how I'd like to pole a keelboat, fully loaded, upstream to KayCee or St. Joe . . .

He became restless, turning his head one way and another . . . the sunlight sparkled on the water, and our legs were all but frozen, so that we were amputated at the knees, the joints set in ice . . .

Back on shore, we shivered, dried ourselves. The sun was past the meridian, the air was already cool. Carl offered me wine, and I drank. Upending the bottle, he finished it in one swallow . . . and, with all his strength, hurled it upstream. Standing together—his hand on my shoulder—we watched it, bobbing in the muddy, choppy waters, floating past us, downstream . . .

We climbed back to the car, and wandered for a while among back roads, circling, until we hit U.S. 40 again, and headed back to St. Louis. Carl was much quieter, his attention abstracted, his face almost morose. He seemed to look—and to drive—without seeing . . .

Reaching St. Charles, we stopped once more, by the river. Carl was stone-faced, immobile, facing upstream . . . when he began to speak, it was in mumbles—to himself, or to no one . . . I knew he was quoting, but I didn't at first know what . . .

> "*Rained the fore part of the day I determined to go as far as St. Charles a french Village 7 Leags. up the Missourie, and wait at that place untill Capt. Lewis could finish the business in which he was obliged to attend to at St. Louis and join me by Land from that place 24 miles*
>
> *I Set out at 4 oClock P.M. in the presence of many of the neighboring inhabitants, and proceeded on under a jentle breese up the Missouri to the upper Point of the 1st Island 4 Miles and camped on the Island which is Situated Close on the right (or Starboard) Side, and opposit the mouth of a Small Creek called Cold water,*
>
> *a heavy rain this afternoon*
>
> "*at 9 oClock Set out and proceeded on 9 miles passed two Islands & incamped on the Starbd. Side at a Mr. Pipers Landing opposet an island, the Boat run on Logs three times to day, owing her being too heavyly loaded a Sturn,*
>
> *a fair after noon, I saw a number of Goslings to day on the Shore, the water excessively rapid, & Banks falling in.*"

... his voice becoming clearer ...

> *"pass a remarkable Coal Hill on the Larboard Side, Called by*
> *the French Carbonere, this hill appear to Contain great quantity*
> *of Coal from this hill the Village of St. Charles may be Seen at*
> *7 miles distance. we arrived at St. Charles at 12 oClock a number*
> *Spectators french & Indians flocked to the bank to See the party.*
> *This Village is about one mile in length, Situated on the north*
> *Side of the Missourie at the foot of a hill from which it takes its*
> *name <u>Peetiete Coete</u> or the <u>Little hill</u> This Village Contns. about*
> *100 houses, the most of them small and indefferent and about 450*
> *inhabitants Chiefly French, those people appear Pore, polite &*
> *harmonious."*

... the opening, the very beginning, of the Journals of Lewis and
Clark ...

We got into the car, and drove to St. Louis.

Coming back to Indianapolis on the train, I reached to an inner coat
pocket for my ticket, and brought out a newspaper clipping. Carl must
have put it there, but I have no idea how or when, or by what sleight
of hand.

It was an obituary:

> "Mills, Maria de la Concepcion—Resident of St. Louis, died in a private
> hospital, after a brief illness. Survivors include the husband, Carl
> Austin Mills, of this city, and a brother, Rico de Castro, with the British
> Royal Air Force, stationed in China."

Holding the clipping before me—the conductor waiting for my ticket
—I was several moments in recalling that a common nickname for
Maria de la Concepcion was Concha ...

On the edge of the clipping, Carl had scribbled a pencil note:

> *"Cancer—in the gut—brutal—"*

F O U R

There was the letter Melville received from an old shipmate:

". . . first of all I will let you know who I am you probably have not forgotten all of the crew of the Old Frigate United States and more especially our visit to the city of Lima. my name is Oliver Russ, although I went by another name when at sea to conceal from my friends the unwise step I had taken and that name was Edward Norton I assumed my right name on coming home. Now what I wish to say is that I in the course of the next year after our return from sea I took to wife one of the fair daughters of the state of Maine and in two years from that day a son was born to us a substantial token of our mutual love and to manifest the high regard in which I have ever held yourself I named him Herman Melville Russ at that time I did not expect ever to hear of you again or that you would be numbered among the literary writers of the day. I say this to let you know that it was not the almost universal desire to name after great men that led me to do it, but a regard for those qualities which an acquaintance of eighteen month with you led me so much to admire."

. . . and on the lists of the 4th voyage, many names appeared—men from Palos and the Niebla—men who had shipped earlier with Columbus . . .

they recalled, perhaps, the storm between Jamaica and Cuba, on the 2nd voyage, when the flagship was hove-to and all hands went below for a rest: the Admiral was the first on deck, and, noting that the weather was moderating, began to make sail himself, so as not to disturb his weary shipmates . . .

Melville: "If ever, in days to come, you shall see ruin at hand, and, thinking you understand mankind, shall tremble for your friendships, and tremble for your pride; and, partly through love for the one and fear for the other, shall resolve to be beforehand with the world, and save it from a sin by prospectively taking that sin to yourself, then will you do as one I now dream of once did, and like him will you suffer; but how fortunate and how grateful should you be, if like him, after all that had happened, you could be a little happy again."

Columbus,

who had always been mysterious about his past, without mother or father, a roving widower—takes a late interest in Genoa:

From the Deed of Entail: "Item. I also enjoin Diego, or any one that may inherit the estate, to have and maintain in the city of Genoa one person of our lineage to reside there with his wife, and appoint him sufficient revenue to enable him to live decently, as a person closely connected with the family, of which he is to be the root and basis in that city; from which great good may accrue to him, inasmuch as I was born there, and came from thence."

". . . and Genoa is a noble city, and powerful by sea . . ."

"I command the said Diego, or whoever may possess the said estate, to labor and strive for the honor, welfare and aggrandizement of the city of Genoa, and make use of all his power and means in defending and enhancing the good and credit of that republic."

Aging, lonely, the Admiral seeks his sources . . .

writing to friends in Genoa: "Although my body is here, my heart is continually yonder."

and to another, just before leaving on the 4th voyage: "The loneliness in which you have left us cannot be described . . . I am ready to start in the name of the Holy Trinity as soon as the weather is good."

and another: "If the desire to hear from you troubles me as much in the places to which I am going, as it does here, I shall feel great anxiety."

On the 4th voyage, heading for Jamaica:

". . . my ships were pierced with worm-holes, like a bee hive, and the crew entirely dispersed and downhearted."

". . . all the people with pumps and kettles and other vessels were insufficient to bail out the water that entered by the worm-holes."

(*Melville: "Bail out your individual boat, if you can, but the sea abides".*

Shore-bound, ship-wrecked, on Jamaica . . .

(*Melville three times underscores, in the*

176

the works of another: "He that is sure of the
goodness of his ship and tackle puts out fear-
lessly from the shore . . ."

(and Melville, on his last sea voyage, age 68
—a pleasure trip to Bermuda: "Rough pass-
age home during blizzard Got around on
hands & knees."

Back in Spain, finished forever with the ocean-sea, Columbus writes
his son Diego:

"Very dear son:

"Since I received your letter of November 15 I have heard
nothing from you. I wish that you would write me more
frequently. I would like to receive a letter from you each
hour. Reason must tell you that I now have no other repose.
Many couriers come each day, and the news is of such a nature and so abundant that in hearing it, all my hair stands
on end, it is so contrary to what my soul desires.

"I told you in that letter that my departure was certain,
but that the hope of my arrival there, according to experience,
was very uncertain, because my sickness is so bad and the
cold is so well suited to aggravate it, that I could not well
avoid remaining in some inn on the road. The litter and
everything were ready. The weather became so violent that it
appeared impossible to every one to start when it was getting
so bad . . .

". . . telling of my sickness and that it is now impossible
for me to go and kiss their Royal feet and hands and that the
Indies are being lost and are on fire in a thousand places, and
that I have received nothing and am receiving nothing from
the revenues derived from them, and that no one dares to
accept or demand anything there for me, and I am living
upon borrowed funds. I spent the money which I got there in
bringing those people who went with me back to their homes,
for it would be a great burden upon my conscience to have
left them there and to have abandoned them.

"Take good care of your brother. He has a good disposition
and is no longer a boy. Ten brothers would not be too many
for you. I never found better friends to right or to left than

my brothers. We must strive to obtain the government of the Indies . . .

"**My illness permits me to write only at night, because in the daytime my hands are deprived of strength.**"

and another time:

"**I wrote a very long letter to his Highness as soon as I arrived here, fully stating the evils which require a prompt and efficient remedy . . . I have received no reply . . .**"

> *(Melville, in a letter, advertises* <u>Clarel</u>: " . . . *a metrical affair . . . eminently adapted for unpopularity.*"

and Columbus signs his letters to Diego, "Your father, who loves you as himself."

as Melville ended a letter to Stanwix: "Good bye, & God bless you, Your affectionate Father, H. Melville."

Melville,

age 69, begins work on Billy Budd, as an afterthought to his life . . .

creates "Starry" Vere, the educated, literary captain, aware (as Melville was) of history and tradition, knowing that their demands must and will be met . . . knowing, too, that the present act is a compound of many elements: out of the hazy near-past, the strong and clear distant-past, and the immediate moment . . .

Melville, as Captain Vere, creates himself a bachelor . . . the old dream!

and creates Billy, the Handsome Sailor—a foundling . . . the old Ishmael dream!

Vere and Billy, bachelor and bastard—the two elements of Melville, split . . .

and Vere it is (as the agent of tradition) who sends Billy to his death . . . Melville, as Vere, thereby accepting responsibility for his son Mackey's death; and perhaps, too, for the death of the Handsome Sailor in himself . . .

or perhaps Billy—pure and merry—was the sexual transposition of Fayaway: the dark savage girl become a pure white man,

> *(*<u>Billy</u>: " . . . *a lingering adolescent expres-*

> sion in the as yet smooth face, all but femi-
> nine in purity of natural complexion ..."

(it being safer to love a man than a woman
...

(as Dreiser transposed himself, saying, in
effect, <u>it is not safe to be myself, I will be
Sister Carrie</u> ...

Melville, an old man, recalls Fayaway ...

> <u>Billy Budd</u>: "In fervid hearts self-contained some brief experi-
> ences devour our human tissue as secret fire in a ship's hold ..."

> and Julian Hawthorne reports an interview with Melville: " ...
> he told me, during our talk, that he was convinced that there was
> some secret in my father's life which had never been revealed, and
> which accounted for the gloomy passages in his books."

Melville—ever the writer—placing things of self in some one else ...

> Mrs. Glendinning, in <u>Pierre</u>: "Oh, that the world were made of
> such malleable stuff, that we could recklessly do our fiercest heart's-
> wish before it ..."

and my hand reaches for a newspaper clipping, the first in a series—
date, 1953:

BOY, 6, IS KIDNAPPED
AT PRIVATE SCHOOL

Son of Wealthy Kansas City
Family Taken by Woman Who
Gave False Story to Nuns

KANSAS CITY, Mo., Sept. 28 (UP)—The 6-year-old son of a wealthy Kansas
City business man was kidnapped from a Roman Catholic school here today by a
woman who represented herself to be the boy's aunt.

The stocky, red-haired woman led Robert C. (Buddy) Williams Jr. from the
French Institute of Notre Dame de Sion after falsely telling the nuns that his
mother had had a heart attack. Hours later the police had been unable to find any
trace of the boy or his abductor.

The child's father is the owner of the only Cadillac automobile agency in Kansas
City, and has similar interests in Oklahoma City and Tulsa, Oklahoma. The family
has a large, English-style home across the state line in Kansas.

The police said that there was no indication whether the kidnapper planned to
seek a ransom.

179

The boy was in the primary grade of the school. He was a half-day pupil and was picked up each school day by the family chauffeur and taken home during the lunch hour. When the chauffeur arrived today the boy was gone.

F I V E

KIDNAPPED BOY FOUND DEAD
AFTER BIG RANSOM IS PAID

Two Jailed
In Missouri

KANSAS CITY, Oct. 8 (AP)—Little Buddy Williams' body was dug out of a shallow grave today, ending with sickening tragedy 10 days of waiting by his wealthy parents who paid a record $600,000 ransom for his return.

Arrested as his kidnappers were the woman who lived in the house in St. Joseph, Mo., where the body was found, and her ex-mental-patient boy friend Carl Austin Mills, 43, whose spending spree in St. Louis led police to part of the ransom money.

The slightly built, 6-year-old boy had been shot and killed the same day the woman, Mrs. Bonnie Brown Heady, 41, took him from his private school by ruse.

The city, the Indiana country around us, are dead quiet. Rising, I find my joints stiff, my body tired. I move around, amble to the end of the attic, loosening my limbs . . .

Carl, stealing a child, attempting by ransom to convert him to his own future,

is a little like Melville—un-centered by the failure of Moby-Dick—clutching Hawthorne: trying to push off on him the "Agatha" story, get him to do Melville's writing:

> ". . . it has occurred to me that this thing lies very much in a vein, with which you are peculiarly familiar. To be plump, I think that in this matter you would make a better hand at it than I would.—Besides the thing seems naturally to gravitate toward you . . ."

> ". . . it seems to me that with your great power in these things, you can construct a story of remarkable interest out of this material

. . . And if I thought I could do it as well as you, why, I should not let you have it."

and, perhaps, like Columbus, before or during the 3rd voyage, writing the Letter to the Nurse . . .

the center-line of communication with the Sovereigns broken: writing, therefore, to an underling, hoping by court gossip to reach the Royal ear . . .

no longer confident . . .

Through the little window in the gable end, I can see only darkness . . . staring through the glass, I think of the 1st voyage, return: Columbus on board the Niña, caught in a violent storm, writing "with caligraphic poise" on a single piece of parchment, trying to reduce to this space the content of his discovery . . . and sealing the parchment in a cask, throwing it overboard . . .

> there was the story that came out of Spain: "At noon of August 27 in the year 1852, an American three-masted brig named the Chieftan, of Boston, under command of Captain d'Auberville, found itself upon the coast of Morocco. As a storm was approaching, the Captain determined to increase his ballast, and while engaged in this occupation, the drag brought up what at first glance appeared to be a piece of rock, but, finding it light in weight, the sailors examined it more closely, when they discovered it to be a coffer of cedar wood: opening this, there was disclosed a cocoa-nut, hollow, and containing a document written in gothic letters upon parchment. Not being able to decipher this, it was given to an American bookseller when the ship arrived at Gibraltar. The latter immediately upon glancing at the manuscript offered the American Captain one hundred dollars for the cocoa-nut and its contents, which offer the Captain declined. Thereupon the bookseller read to the astonished Captain the document, which was no other than the holograph relation of the discovery committed to the sea three hundred and fifty-nine years before." . . . but the fictional parchment disappeared . . .

> and, likewise, "My Secrete Log Boke"—a "facsimile edition" of a version found by a fisherman off the coast of Wales—printed in English, the "universal maritime language"—and appropriately adorned with barnacles and seaweed.

but—in fact—there was Raymond Weaver—first of Melville scholars—who, in 1919, dug loose the tin bread box from the tight seaweed of Melville's heirs and descendants, and brought out the crabbed, incoherent manuscript of Billy Budd . . .

I think of Isabella, first permanent settlement in the Indies—swept by
epidemic, poverty and starvation, and rapidly depopulated . . .

> "It was also said . . . that one day one man or two were walking amidst
> those buildings of Isabella when, in a street, there suddenly appeared two
> rows or choruses of men, who seemed to be noble and court people, well
> dressed, with swords girt and wrapped in traveling cloaks of the kind
> worn in Spain in those days, and when that person or those persons were
> wondering how such people so new and well dressed had landed there . . .
> on asking them whence they came, they answered silently by putting
> their hands to their hats to greet them and, when they took their hats
> off, their heads came off also and they remained headless, and then
> vanished: of which vision the man or men were left nearly dead and for
> many days pained and astonished."

and the Naval expedition, in the year 1891—the year of Melville's
death:

> "Commander G. A. Converse,
>
> "Commanding U. S. S. Enterprise.
>
> "Sir:—
>
> "In obedience to your orders of the 13th inst. we respectfully submit
> the following report of the results of an exploration of the ruins of the
> city of Isabella.
>
> "The party left the Enterprise, then anchored off Puerto Plata, Island
> of Santo Domingo, at 6.30 on the morning of the 14th of May and pro-
> ceeded in the steamcutter thirty miles to the westward along the north
> shore of the island of Santo Domingo. We were accompanied by an old
> native pilot who was recommended by the U. S. Consul of Puerto Plata
> as familiar with the coast and such traditions as exist among the natives
> respecting the first settlement of Columbus. He has piloted vessels to and
> from the port of Isabella for many years.
>
> "About eight miles inside the cape now known as Isabella there is a
> bay of considerable size; on its easter shore a slight rocky projection of
> land formed by one of the numerous bluffs was chosen for the first
> permanent settlement of the Spaniards in the New World . . .
>
> "No habitations are to be found within a mile and a half of the ruins . . .
>
> "On landing we turned to the right and ascended a gentle slope to a
> little plain about two acres in area; this slightly projects into the bay and
> is bounded on the north and south by two dry water-courses forming
> natural ditches, or moats, and terminating abruptly on the western, or
> water side, in cliffs from twenty to thirty feet high formed by large
> boulders containing fossil coral and shells. Tradition points to this little
> plateau as the site of the ancient city and here we found scattered at
> intervals various small, ill-defined heaps of stones, remnants of walls
> built of small unhewn stones, evidently laid in mortar, pieces of old tiles
> and potsherds, some of the latter glazed, and fragments of broad, roughly

made bricks. There were half a dozen or more blocks of dressed limestone that may have been part of the walls of buildings somewhat finished and permanent in character. The trees, matted roots and trailing vines overspread the ground . . .

"We overturned all the cut blocks of stone and examined them carefully in the hope of finding some marks or dates, but without success, and it is our belief that nothing of the kind exists.

"Should further exploration be made it would be of undoubted scientific interest to examine the fauna and flora of this region and there are evidences of interesting fossil remains. The caves in the cliffs of Cape Isabella and vicinity would probably yield interesting relics of the aborigines—the now extinct Caribs."

Melville—Customs Inspector #75—writes a letter to John Hoadley: "By the way I have a ship on my district from Girgenti— Where's that? Why, in Sicily—The ancient Agrigentum. Ships arrive from there in this port, bringing sulphur; but this is the first one I have happened to have officially to do with. I have not succeeded in seeing the captain yet—have only seen the mate— but hear that he has in possession some stones from those magnificent Grecian ruins, and I am going to try to get a fragment, however small, if possible, which I will divide with you."

and Isabella today: a pasture by the sea, with only a few stones above the ground . . .

Turning, I amble back to the desk . . .

WOMAN WHO LURED BOY FROM SCHOOL
TELLS POLICE HE WASN'T FRIGHTENED

ST. LOUIS, Oct. 7 (AP)—The woman who lured Buddy Williams from his school in Kansas City on the start of a trip that was to lead to a shallow grave said today the 6-year-old boy wasn't frightened.

"He was such a sweet child," said Mrs. Bonnie Brown Heady.

"He came so nice. He talked about getting a dog and ice cream."

> (and there was Billy Budd: ". . . he showed in face that humane look of reposeful good nature . . ."

> ("The ear, small and shapely, the arch of the foot, the curve in mouth and nostril . . ."

> (and he was called by his shipmates, Baby Budd . . .

PAIR PLEAD GUILTY
TO KIDNAP CHARGE

KANSAS CITY, Nov. 3 (AP)—Ex-mental patient Carl Austin Mills and his alcoholic companion, Mrs. Bonnie Brown Heady, pleaded guilty in federal court today to the kidnapping of 6-year-old Buddy Williams and were ordered to trial Nov. 16.

we thought that, because of his mental record, he would plead insanity, and all of us—Mother, Linda and I—tried to persuade him to it; but Carl himself insisted against it, and such a plea was never made . . . instead, he took a rigorous psychiatric examination, and conned his way through it . . .

KIDNAP KILLERS WILL DIE
DEC. 18; 'TOO GOOD FOR
THEM,' WILLIAMS SAYS

Mrs. Hall,
Mills Stoically
Hear Sentence

KANSAS CITY, Nov. 19 (AP)—The kidnap slayers of Buddy Williams were sentenced to death today and will go to the gas chamber together for their ruthless crime.

I made several trips—to St. Louis, Kansas City, Jefferson City—but on all occasions Carl refused to see me, or acknowledge me . . .

PENITENTIARY GATES
CLOSE ON KIDNAPPERS

No Appeals Planned

JEFFERSON CITY, Mo., Nov. 20 (AP)—The Buddy Williams kidnap killers reached the Missouri Penitentiary tonight where they will die together in the gas chamber one week from Christmas.

Carl Austin Mills, 43, and Mrs. Bonnie Brown Heady, 41, were received at the grim gray-walled prison in gathering darkness at 5.35 p.m. They arrived in handcuffs and chains after an automobile trip from Kansas City . . .

On Thursday, the 20th of May, 1506, in the city of Valladolid, Christopher Columbus died . . .

(Melville:

("*Like those new-world discoverers bold
Ending in stony convent cold,*

Or dying hermits; as if they,

.   .   .   .

> *Remorseful felt that ampler sway*
> *Their lead had given for old career*
> *Of human nature."*

and Melville, in 1891, the year of his death, set aside Billy Budd, as finished—and picked it up again: added a chapter—afterthought to an afterthought—Billy In The Darbies:

> *". . . Sentry, are you there?*
> *Just ease these darbies at the wrist,*
> *And roll me over fair.*
> *I am sleepy . . ."*

There was the editor of the Atlantic Monthly, discussing a possible article on Melville:

> *"I can't help thinking that there must be some good material on the subject, though probably it would be better still if Melville would only let go of life. So much more frankness of speech can be used when a fellow is apparently out of hearing. What you say of his aversion to publicity makes me pause . . .*
>
> *"On second thought therefore, I believe we had better wait for our shot at Melville, when his personality can be more freely handled."*

. . . like Ovando, sending a ship to rescue Columbus on Jamaica: standing off shore, hovering, hoping him dead . . .

and Melville writes Daniel Orme:

> *"But let us come to the close of a sketch necessarily imperfect. One fine Easter Day, following a spell of rheumatic weather, Orme was discovered alone and dead on a height overlooking the seaward sweep of the great haven to whose shore, in his retirement from sea, he had moored. It was an evened terrace, destined for use in war, but in peace neglected and offering a sanctuary for anybody. Mounted on it was an obsolete battery of rusty guns. Against one of these he was found leaning, his legs stretched out before him; his clay pipe broken in twain, the vacant bowl and no spillings from it, attesting that his pipe had been smoked out to the last of its contents. He faced the outlet to the ocean. The eyes were open, still continuing in death the vital glance fixed on the hazy waters and the dim-seen sails coming and going or at anchor near by. What*

had been his last thoughts! If aught of reality lurked in the ru-
mours concerning him, had remorse, had penitence any place in
those thoughts? Or was there just nothing of either? After all,
were his moodiness and mutterings, his strange freaks, starts,
eccentric shrugs and grimaces, were these but the grotesque addi-
tions like the wens and knobs and distortions of the trunk of an
old chance apple-tree in an inclement upland, not only beaten by
many storms, but also obstructed in its natural development by the
chance of its having first sprouted among hard-packed rock? In
short, that fatality, no more encrusting him, made him what he
came to be? Even admitting that there was something dark that
he chose to keep to himself, what then? Such reticence may some-
times be more for the sake of others than one's self. No, let us
believe that the animal decay before mentioned still befriended
him to the close, and that he fell asleep recalling through the haze
of memory many a far-off scene of the wide world's beauty
dreamily suggested by the hazy waters before him.

"He lies buried among other sailors, for whom also strangers
performed one last rite in a lonely plot overgrown with wild eglan-
tine uncared for by man."

and on the 28th of September, 1891, Melville—unwilling to face another northern winter—died . . .

there was the dedication of <u>Billy Budd</u>: to an old shipmate, Jack Chase,
"wherever that great heart may now be . . ."

and Melville's physician signed the certificate, ascribing death to "Car-
diac dilitation . . ."

ENLARGEMENT OF THE HEART

I get up, stand by the desk, and turn off the light. A thin bit of gray
comes through the attic window. There is a strange smell of gas, sulphurous, that I had smelled earlier, much earlier in the evening . . .

WILLIAMS KIDNAPPERS
DIE SIDE BY SIDE IN
MISSOURI GAS CHAMBER

Mrs. Heady,
Mills Chat
Before Death

From UP And AP Reports

JEFFERSON CIT Y, Mo., Friday, Dec. 18—Bonnie Heady and Carl Mills died side by side in a swirl of poison gas early today for kidnapping a little boy and killing him.

In the last hours before they were taken to the death house, the killers had kept a strange composure.

. . . deadly fumes with the faint scent of almonds.

the daylight is getting stronger . . .

treading softly, I go downstairs, both flights, and into the kitchen. I stand by the table, resting one hand on it, trying to listen to the silence. The refrigerator motor turns on, becomes a steady hum. I hear one of the children, Jenifer, stirring . . .

BIBLIOGRAPHY

Arey, Leslie Brainard—Developmental Anatomy (3rd Edition, Revised)
Associated Press Accounts—Bobby Greenlease Kidnapping Story
———— Sullivan County (Indiana) Mine Disaster
Berrill, N. J.—The Signs Columbus Followed (in *Natural History*, October, 1950)
Bjorkman, Edwin—The Search For Atlantis
Blakiston's New Gould Medical Dictionary
Bondi, H.—Cosmology
Carden, Robert W.—The City of Genoa
Catt, C. C. & Shuler, N. R.—Woman Suffrage And Politics
The Cyclopedia of Medicine, Surgery and Specialties—1949 Edition
de Madariaga, Salvador—Christopher Columbus
DeVoto, Bernard (editor)—The Journals of Lewis and Clark
Dreiser, Theodore—Sister Carrie
Eggleston, Edward—The Hoosier Schoolmaster
Elias, Robert H.—Theodore Dreiser: Apostle of Nature
Encyclopaedia Britannica—1946 Edition
Ford, P. L. (editor)—Writings of Christopher Columbus
Goss, Charles Mayo, M.D. (editor)—Gray's Anatomy of The Human Body (25th
   Edition)
Homer—The Odyssey (Samuel Butler translation)
Hubbard, L. Ron—Dianetics: The Modern Science of Mental Health
———— subsequent books, articles, etc., on Dianetics and Scientology
Indiana Writers' Project—Indiana: A Guide To The Hoosier State
Irving, Washington—The Life And Voyages Of Columbus
Jameson, J. F. (editor)—Original Narratives of The Voyages of Columbus
Jones, William—Credulities Past and Present
Jordan, Harvey Ernest & Kindred, James Ernest—A Textbook of Embryology
Leyda, Jay—The Melville Log
Martindale, Ramona—Unpublished manuscripts, letters, etc.
May, Alan G.—Mummies from Alaska (in *Natural History*, March, 1951)
Melville, Herman—The Apple-Tree Table
———— Bartleby The Scrivener
———— Benito Cereno
———— Billy Budd, Foretopman
———— Clarel
———— Collected Poems
———— The Confidence-Man
———— Daniel Orme

———— The Encantadas, or Enchanted Isles
———— Fragments From A Writing Desk
———— The Happy Failure
———— Hawthorne And His Mosses
———— I And My Chimney
———— Israel Potter
———— Journal Of A Visit To London And The Continent
———— Journal Up The Straits
———— Mardi
———— Moby-Dick
———— Omoo
———— Paradise Of Bachelors
———— The Piazza
———— Pierre
———— Redburn
———— Tartarus Of Maids
———— The Two Temples
———— Typee
———— White-Jacket
Metcalf, Eleanor Melville—Herman Melville, Cycle And Epicycle
Milne, E. A.—Kinematic Relativity
Missouri Writers' Project—Missouri: A Guide To The "Show Me" State
Morison, Samuel Eliot—Admiral Of The Ocean-Sea
Murray, Henry A.—Notes to Melville's *Pierre*
National Geographic Society—The Book of Fishes
Olson, Charles—Call Me Ishmael
Plato—The Timaeus
———— The Critias
Ragozin, Zenaide A.—A History Of The World—Earliest Peoples
Roberts, John D.—Personal letters
Shipley, Joseph T.—Dictionary Of Word Origins
Spence, Lewis—Atlantis In America
———— History Of Atlantis
Thacher, John Boyd—Christopher Columbus
United Press Accounts—Bobby Greenlease Kidnapping Story
Vaillant, George C.—Indian Arts In North America
Vestal, Stanley—The Missouri (Rivers of America Series)
von Hagen, Victor W.—Shrunken Heads (in *Natural History*, March, 1952)
Willy, A., Vander, L., & Fisher, O.—The Illustrated Encyclopedia Of Sex
Yates, Raymond—The Weather As A Hobby